His hand slid up under the hem of Delilah's jacket and crept beneath her thermal sweater until his cool fingers traced over the hot skin of her waist. "Kiss me."

She lowered her mouth to his slowly, her heart pounding. His lips were warm and dry, soft at first, but hardening as her mouth met his. She threaded her fingers through his dark hair, slanting his head so that their mouths fit together more completely.

Kissing him still felt like sin and salvation, contradictory and irresistible. She knew she couldn't let herself want him, but she was powerless to resist the pull of attraction. Nothing— not their present danger or their past betrayals— could stem the tide of her desire...

Dear Harlequin Intrigue Reader,

For nearly thirty years fearless romance has fueled every Harlequin Intrigue book. Now we want everyone to know about the great crime stories our fantastic authors write and the variety of compelling miniseries we offer. We think our new cover look complements and enhances our promise to deliver edge-of-your-seat reads in all six of our titles—and brand-new titles every month!

This month's lineup is packed with nonstop mystery in *Smoky Ridge Curse,* the third in Paula Graves's Bitterwood P.D. trilogy, exciting action in *Sharpshooter,* the next installment in Cynthia Eden's Shadow Agents miniseries, and of course fearless romance—whether from newcomers Jana DeLeon and HelenKay Dimon or veteran author Aimée Thurlo, we've got every angle covered.

Next month buckle up as Debra Webb returns with a new Colby Agency series featuring The Specialists. And in November *USA TODAY* bestselling author B.J. Daniels takes us back to "The Canyon" for her special *Christmas at Cardwell Ranch* celebration.

Lots going on and lots more to come. Be sure to check out www.Harlequin.com for what's coming next.

Enjoy,

Denise Zaza

Senior Editor

Harlequin Intrigue

SMOKY RIDGE CURSE

—

PAULA GRAVES

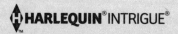

HARLEQUIN® INTRIGUE®

For my readers, who choose to read my stories when
there's such a delightful array of great books out
there to be enjoyed. I'm forever grateful.

Recycling programs
for this product may
not exist in your area.

ISBN-13: 978-0-373-69705-2

SMOKY RIDGE CURSE

Copyright © 2013 by Paula Graves

Printed in U.S.A.

www.Harlequin.com

ABOUT THE AUTHOR

Alabama native Paula Graves wrote her first book, a mystery starring herself and her neighborhood friends, at the age of six. A voracious reader, Paula loves books that pair tantalizing mystery with compelling romance. When she's not reading or writing, she works as a creative director for a Birmingham advertising agency and spends time with her family and friends. She is a member of Southern Magic Romance Writers, Heart of Dixie Romance Writers and Romance Writers of America.

Paula invites readers to visit her website, www.paulagraves.com.

Books by Paula Graves

HARLEQUIN INTRIGUE

*Cooper Justice
**Cooper Justice: Cold Case Investigation
‡Cooper Security
‡‡Bitterwood P.D.

CAST OF CHARACTERS

Delilah Hammond—The Bitterwood, Tennessee, native has returned home after years away. But when her former boss—and onetime lover—shows up injured and on the run from the good guys and bad guys alike, she realizes she has to face her past before she can plan her future.

Adam Brand—Once a rising star in the FBI, Brand is a hunted man, framed for espionage and murder. With pursuers closing in, he goes to the only person he trusts, his former protégée, Delilah.

Wayne Cortland—The lumberyard owner seems to be an upstanding businessman in his rural Virginia town. Is Brand right that his law-abiding facade is a clever cover for a ruthless backwoods crime lord?

Rachel Davenport—Her stepbrother tried to kill her shortly after he met with a man fitting Wayne Cortland's description. Could Cortland be the one targeting her for murder?

Seth Hammond—Though Delilah's brother has reformed his wicked ways, someone's still gunning for him. Are his troubles connected to his checkered past? Or has his relationship with Rachel Davenport made him a target?

Nolan Cavanaugh—The geeky code cracker has helped catch criminals before. But is he working against Wayne Cortland—or for him?

Glen Rayburn—The Bitterwood police department's captain of detectives has proved an impediment to recent police investigations. Is he digging in his heels against changes in the department, or are his motives darker?

Alexander Quinn—What does the CIA master spy want from Adam Brand? Does he know more about Wayne Cortland's criminal enterprise than he's willing to say? And who is the mystery man he's sent to keep track of Brand's movements?

Chapter One

Winter had come to Bitterwood, Tennessee, roaring in on a cold, damp wind that poured down the mountain passes and shook the remnants of browning leaves from the sugar maples, sweet gums and dogwoods growing at the middle elevations. Delilah Hammond remembered well from childhood the sharp bite of an Appalachian November and dressed warmly when she headed up the winding mountain road to her mother's place on Smoky Ridge.

Reesa Hammond was on day three of her latest hop on the sobriety wagon, and withdrawal had hit her hard, killing her appetite and leaving her shaking, angry and suffering from a persistent headache no amount of ibuprofen seemed to relieve. Frankly, Delilah was surprised her mother had bothered trying to stop drinking at all at this point, since her previous eight attempts at sobriety had all ended the same way, five fingers deep in a bottle of Jack Daniel's whiskey.

Delilah didn't kid herself that this time Reesa would win the battle with the bottle. But Reesa had taken a hell of a lot of abuse trying to protect Delilah and her brother, Seth, from their sick creep of a sperm donor, so a little barley soup and a few minutes of company wasn't too much to offer, was it?

Her cell phone beeped as she turned her Camaro into a tight curve. She waited until the road straightened to answer, aware of how dangerous the mountain roads could be, especially at night with rain starting to mix with sleet. "Hammond."

"Just checking to make sure you hadn't changed your mind." The gruff voice on the other end of the line belonged to a former leatherneck named Jesse Cooper, the man who'd been her boss for the past few years, until she'd given her notice two weeks earlier.

"I haven't," she answered, tamping down the doubts that had harassed her ever since she'd quit the best job she'd ever had.

"You're overqualified."

"I know."

"You're no good at small-town politics."

"I know that, too."

"You should have held out for chief of police, at least."

She grinned at that. "Talk about small-town politics."

"I can keep the job open for a month or two, but that's it. Our caseload's growing, and I can't afford to work short-handed."

"I know. I appreciate the vote of confidence in me, but I'm ready for a change." She tried not to dwell on just how drastic a change she'd made in the past two weeks. Going from a global security and threat assessment firm to a detective on one of Tennessee's tiniest police forces was turning out to be a shock to the system even she hadn't anticipated.

She still wasn't sure why, exactly, she'd decided to stick around Bitterwood, Tennessee, after so many years away. She only knew that a few weeks ago, when the time had come to go back to work in Alabama after an extended assignment in her old hometown, her feet had planted firmly in the rocky Tennessee soil and refused to budge. She'd returned to Maybridge just long enough to work out her two-week notice, talk her landlord into letting her break her long-term lease and gather up her sparse belongings. Two days ago, she'd moved into a rental house off Vesper Road at the foot of Smoky Ridge. In a week, she'd start her new job with the Bitterwood Police Department.

"I don't suppose you've heard anything else about Adam Brand?" she added as the silence between her and her former boss lingered past comfort.

"Nothing yet. We have feelers out. I know you're worried."

"Not worried," she denied, though it was a lie. "More confused than anything. Going AWOL is not an Adam Brand kind of thing to do. And there's no way in hell he's a traitor to this country. It's not in his DNA."

"Your brother still won't tell you anything more about the work he did for Brand?"

"I don't think Seth knows anything more," Delilah said. "He didn't ask a lot of questions, and Brand's not one to shoot off his mouth." Even when a few well-chosen words might do him a world of good, she added silently.

"Isabel and Ben have both been trying to reach him, but they're not having much luck. They didn't keep in close touch with Brand after leaving the bureau."

"It happens." Delilah ignored the stinging pain in the center of her chest. "I've got to go. I'm taking soup and sympathy to my mom. She's on the wagon again."

"Oh." She could tell by Jesse's careful tone that he wanted to say something encouraging, but he'd been around for three or four of her mother's last brief flirtations with sobriety and knew better than to dish out false hope. "I hope she makes it this time."

"Yeah, me, too. Say hi to everyone. And call me if you get any news about Brand. I don't think this Davenport case is really over yet, and he seems to know something about it."

"Will do." Jesse hung up.

The Davenport case was at least part of the reason she'd stuck around Bitterwood. Two months earlier, the murders had started—four women found stabbed to death in their beds, though they'd clearly been killed elsewhere. A Bitterwood P.D. detective named Ivy Hawkins had made the first clear connection between the murders—all four women had been friends with a woman named Rachel Davenport, whose dying father owned Davenport Trucking in Maryville, Tennessee, a town twenty minutes from Bitterwood.

When Ivy had caught the murderer, he'd admitted he'd been hired to kill the women. With his cryptic dying words, he'd hinted the killings had everything to do with Rachel Davenport, as Ivy had suspected. Someone had wanted to torment Rachel until she broke, and only after several close calls had the police discovered a struggle for control of Davenport Trucking was at the heart of the campaign of emotional torture.

If there was anything good to come out of the whole mess, it was that Delilah's black sheep of a brother, Seth, had ended up a hero and even won the girl—he and Rachel Davenport were already talking rings and wedding dates, which seemed pretty quick to Delilah. Then again, she was thirty-four and single. Some might say she was a little too cautious about affairs of the heart.

Her mother's house was a small cabin near the summit of Smoky Ridge, prone to power outages when the winter storms rolled in. But she had a large fireplace in the front room and a smaller woodstove to warm her bedroom, both of which seemed to be working based on the twin columns of smoke rising over the fir trees surrounding the small cabin.

A thin layer of sleet had started to form on the hard surface of the narrow driveway next to the cabin, crunching under Delilah's boots as she crossed the tiny concrete patio to the kitchen entrance. She had to bend into the wind as it gusted past her, slapping the screen door against the wall of the cabin.

It swung back as she passed, crashing into her with an aluminum rattle.

She stopped short, skidding on the icy pellets underfoot, and stared at the offending screen door. It hung sideways, still flapping in the cold wind, as if someone had tried to rip it from its hinges.

Moving slowly, she stepped back and reached into her pocket for her keychain, where she kept a small flashlight attached to the ring. She snapped it on and ran the narrow beam across the patio beneath the door.

Dark red splotches, still wet and glistening beneath the thin layer of sleet, marred the concrete surface. Another streak of red stained the aluminum frame of the broken door.

Her first thought was that her mother had gone back on the bottle, taken a spill and was laid up inside somewhere, drunkenly trying to patch herself up. It was the most logical assumption.

But a lot of bad things had been happening in Bitterwood in the past couple of months. And between her FBI training and her years working for Cooper Security, Delilah always assumed the worst.

Setting the bag of take-out soup on the patio table, she pulled her Sig Sauer P229 from the pancake holster behind her back and tried the back doorknob. Unlocked.

She eased the door open. Heat blasted her, a welcome contrast to the icy breeze prickling the exposed skin of her neck. Somewhere in the house, a vacuum cleaner was running on high, its whine almost drowning out the whistle of the wind across the eaves.

She shut the door quietly. Keeping her eyes and ears open, she moved as silently as she could, checking each room as she went. If there had been blood splotches inside the house, they'd been cleaned up already. The rough wood floor beneath her feet was worn but spotless.

In the den at the front of the house, the sound of the vacuum cleaner roared with full force. Reesa Hammond was running an upright vacuum with cheerful energy, dancing to whatever tune she was singing beneath the noise of the cleaner.

She swirled the cleaner around in the opposite direction and jumped when she saw Delilah standing in the doorway, weapon in hand.

Reesa shut off the vacuum cleaner and put her hand over her chest. "Good Lord, Dee Dee, you scared me out of my wits!"

"Are you okay?"

Reesa's brow furrowed. "I'm fine. Are *you* okay?"

After a pause, Delilah reholstered her Sig Sauer. "Did you know the screen door to the kitchen's been nearly ripped off its hinges?"

"Really?" Reesa looked surprised. "It was fine when I got back from the mailbox this afternoon. I guess the wind's stronger out there than I thought."

"I don't think it was the wind," Delilah murmured, remembering the blood on the patio. "You didn't hear anything?"

"I was in the shower for a little while, then running the hair dryer, and I've been vacuuming the place ever since. I reckon half the mountain could have come down out there and I wouldn't have heard it." She cocked her head. "You look tired."

Delilah gazed back at her mother through narrowed eyes. "I thought you were feeling bad."

Reesa looked sheepish. "I was, this morning. But when you called and said you were coming over, I didn't want you to see what a mess the place was, so I started cleaning up. And before I knew it, my headache was gone, and I was feeling so much like my old self, I thought maybe I'd surprise you by having dinner ready for you when you got here." She sighed. "But you're early. I haven't put the casserole in the oven yet."

"I brought barley soup from Ledbetter's Café." And left it out in the cold, she realized, where it had probably reached refrigerator temperature by now.

"And I've ruined it for you by feeling better." Reesa patted her cheek. "I'm sorry. I know I must seem such a mess to you."

Unexpected tears burned Delilah's eyes. She blinked them away. "I'm just glad you're feeling better."

Reesa's smile faded. "This is the farthest I've gotten, you know? I've never reached the point where I actually feel better not drinking. It's a surprise, I have to say!"

"Well, good." Delilah couldn't keep a hint of caution out of her voice. She could tell her mother didn't miss the inflection, for Reesa's green eyes darkened with shame for a moment.

But she lifted her chin and smiled at her daughter. "I think it's havin' my kids around me again. I've missed you both so much."

"Seth's been by?" Delilah asked as her mother unplugged the vacuum cleaner and started looping the cord around the hooks in the back.

"He stopped in with Rachel earlier today." Reesa slanted a quick look at Delilah. "She's good for him."

"She's great for him," Delilah agreed. "She's crazy about him, too. Go figure."

"What about you?" Putting the vacuum cleaner away in the living room closet, Reesa paused to look over her shoulder. "Met anyone you like?"

"Not recently," Delilah answered. Actually, she'd met her share of men over the course of working for Cooper Security, but none who'd interested her enough to keep seeing him long-term.

There was only one man she'd ever really wanted, and though he'd never be hers, she still seemed to measure every man she met against him.

"Maybe you'll meet someone when you start work."

"Maybe," Delilah agreed in order to end this particular topic of conversation. She'd already met everyone in the Bitterwood Police Department without a single spark flying. Most were married, and of those who weren't, only Antoine Parsons was remotely interesting. But he was seeing someone in Maryville, and Delilah had never been a poacher.

Even when the man she wanted was married to his career.

"I can put the casserole in the freezer and make it some other time, since you brought soup." Reesa nudged Delilah down the hall to the kitchen.

"No, the soup will keep in the fridge. I'm curious to see this casserole you've cooked up." Delilah spotted a foil-covered glass casserole dish sitting by the refrigerator. She sneaked a peek under the foil, recognizing green beans, carrots, chicken chunks and whole-kernel yellow corn, topped with cheese and fried onions. "You made pantry casserole!" She turned to her mother, a smile playing at her lips.

"I didn't have much in the pantry, but I thought it would be nice to fix something for you." Reesa's smile held a hint of apology. "Maybe next time you come, I'll go shopping first and make something from scratch instead of out of cans."

Impulsively, Delilah hugged her mother. "Pantry casserole is my favorite. I make it at home all the time."

Reesa's thin arms tightened around Delilah's back. "You do?"

"I do. Can't go wrong—"

"—with a casserole," Reesa finished in unison with her.

"I'll go outside and get the soup. You get that in the oven and then we can talk while it's cooking." Delilah let go of her mother and opened the back door. "Mom, you need to start locking your door."

"Nobody ever bothers me up here."

"Famous last words," Delilah muttered as she stepped out onto the sleet-pebbled patio to fetch the soup.

But the paper bag was gone.

Delilah froze, scanning the area behind the house for any sign of an intruder. Visibility wasn't great, between the steady needling of sleet and the cold mist swallowing the top of the mountain. Seeing nothing out of place, she pulled out her flashlight and checked the ground around the patio table. No sign of the bag of take-out soup, but the layer of sleet on the patio had been disturbed.

She couldn't say the streaks of bare patio were definitely footsteps—she supposed it was more likely that a hungry raccoon or opossum had grabbed himself a ready-made meal— but a thin film of blood on the edge of the table was troubling enough to send her reaching for her Sig again.

"Hello?" she called, loudly enough that a faint echo of her voice rang back to her from deep in the woods.

No answer.

The cabin door opened behind her, making her jump. "Dee Dee, is something wrong?"

"The soup is gone."

"Oh." Reesa looked nonplussed.

"Probably a raccoon or something."

"Hope it's not a bear." Reesa shuddered. "Pam Colby said she saw a black bear in her backyard just last week, looking for a place to nest for the winter. She shooed it off by banging some pots together."

"I don't think it's a bear." Delilah's gaze settled on the film of blood. "I'm going to take a look around, okay? I'll be back in a few minutes."

"It's freezing out there. I'm sure it was just an animal,

Dee. Why don't you come back in here where it's warm? Let the raccoon have the soup. He probably needs it more than we do."

"I'm just going to walk the perimeter. There's some blood on the table—maybe it's injured and needs help."

"Oh, poor thing. Okay, but hurry up. The temperature's dropping like crazy out here. They're talking about maybe our first snow of the season." Reesa backed into the house, closing the door behind her.

Stamping her feet to get some of the feeling back into her cold toes, Delilah headed out into the yard, keeping the beam of the flashlight moving in a slow, thorough arc in front of her.

She discovered more blood, spattered on the grass in a weaving line toward the tree line. Following the trail, she spotted a white birch tree with a dark streak of red marring its papery bark about four feet up. The mark seemed to form a long fingerprint.

She paused and checked the magazine of her pistol, reassuring herself that the Sig was loaded, with a round already chambered. If her mother was right and their intruder was a bear, she didn't want to face it unarmed.

Though she listened carefully for any sounds that might reveal an animal or other intruder nearby, all she heard was the moan of the icy wind through the trees. But she felt something else there. Something living and watching, waiting for her to turn around and leave.

What would happen if she did just that? Would the watcher let her go? Or would he pounce the second she turned her back? Not caring to find out, she backed toward the clearing with slow, steady steps. She kept her eyes on the woods, trying to see past the moonless blackness outside the narrow, weakening beam of her flashlight.

Only the faintest of snapping sounds behind her gave her any warning at all.

It wasn't enough.

She hit a solid wall of heat. One large arm curled around her, pulling her flush against that heat, while a hand closed over her mouth.

"Don't scream," he growled.

She didn't.

But he did.

Chapter Two

Pain gutted him, ripping its way around his wounded side and settling like liquid fire in the center of his stomach. He tried to keep his hold on her, tried to bite back the cry that tore from his throat as she slammed her elbow back into his side again.

"Delilah, stop." Adam Brand stumbled backward, struggling to keep his feet as his body instinctively sought relief from her lethal limbs.

A second later, he was staring down the barrel of her Sig Sauer P229 backlit by the beam of a flashlight.

"Son of a bitch!" Delilah hit the last word hard and dropped the weapon and flashlight to her side, bending nearly double as if she'd been the one to take the blow to the gut. "You scared the hell out of me, Brand."

"I think you reopened my wound," Brand shot back, his voice hoarse with pain. He pressed his hand to his side and found that the wound, which had finally started to clot, was weeping blood again.

"Your wound?" Delilah straightened quickly, swinging the beam of her flashlight over him, searching for his injury.

He turned his side toward her helpfully. "I think it was a thirty-two. I got lucky."

In the low light of the flashlight beam, her pretty face twisted with a grimace. "Lucky, huh?" She plucked at his shirt, making him wince as the cotton clung to the drying blood around the bullet furrow. "Where the hell have you been? The police are looking for you."

"I know. That's why I didn't knock on the door."

"What did you do with my soup?"

"Ate it," Brand admitted. "I haven't had anything to eat besides what I could forage for a couple of days."

Delilah's sharp brown eyes lifted to meet his. "The FBI says you're a traitor."

"You know better." At least, he hoped she did. A lot of time had passed since they'd last seen each other.

People changed.

"What happened? How did it get to this point?" Her eyes narrowed. "Does it have anything to do with the Davenport case?"

"It's connected," he said. "But it's a lot more complicated than that." He tried to hold back a shiver, but the wind at his back was too damned icy for him to stop shaking.

Delilah's brow furrowed. "We need to get you inside and warmed up."

"I can't go in there. Your mother's there."

"You don't have a choice. If you stay out here much longer, you'll go into hypothermia. Here." She took off her jacket and handed it to him.

Brand looked at the thick denim jacket, built to hug her smaller frame. "That's not going to fit me."

She gave him an exasperated look, one he'd seen a thousand times before and had feared he might never see again. Cold, hungry and hurting, he still felt a crushing need to pull her close and say all the things he'd never said, to hell with his reasons for choosing the path he had. But now was no better time than the other times he'd stayed silent and let the moment pass.

"Wrap it around your neck to block the wind," she said flatly. "I take it you don't want to be found?"

The pragmatism of her question made him smile. It felt as if his face cracked into a million pieces at the effort. "That would be best."

"I'll make an excuse to my mother about why I have to go. Here." She dug in the pocket of her jeans and handed him a set of keys. "Get in my car and lie down in the backseat. It should still be fairly warm. But don't start the engine. I don't want my mother suspicious."

She started toward the small cabin with the cheery golden light in the windows and fragrant wood smoke wafting from the chimney, moving with long, kinetic strides that reminded him of those days, so many years ago, when she'd brought energy and life to his little section of the federal government.

He couldn't say she hadn't changed since that time—eight years of life had chiseled away the softness of her features, honing them to a mature, womanly beauty. And her eyes seemed, if anything, darker and more mysterious than he remembered, as if in leaving the FBI behind she'd also abandoned the openness of youth.

Brand trudged over the frozen ground to the low-slung black Camaro he'd seen her park just a little while earlier. At least she hadn't lost her sense of style, he thought with a weak grin as he opened the car and bent to push up the bucket seat so he could crawl into the back. Stretching out on the narrow backseat, with its console hump in the middle, he changed his mind, wishing she'd grown staid enough to drive a roomy four-door sedan with a bench seat in the back.

At least inside the car he was sheltered from the biting wind and sleet, and the stinging numbness in his fingers and toes eased. For the first time in days, he closed his eyes and relaxed, enjoying the relative comfort of civilization while he could.

Sometime later, the crunch of footsteps on the ground outside jerked him out of a light doze. He tensed until the driver's-side door opened and Delilah slid into the car. "Still alive?" she drawled as she buckled her seat belt. Her Appalachian accent had gotten stronger during her time away, he noticed.

"Barely."

"You're not bleedin' on my seat, are you?"

Brand grinned. "No."

"Who shot you?" she asked.

"I'm not sure."

She was silent for a moment, as if deciding whether or not to believe him. "Okay, who ordered you shot?"

Not much got past her. "I can't prove it, but the only person I've made an enemy of lately is a man named Wayne Cortland."

"Cortland." She rolled the name around in her mouth the way only a mountain girl could do. "Never heard of him."

"Believe me, that's by design."

She cranked the car and set the heat up to high. Warm air wafted almost immediately into the back, and he sighed with relief.

"I'm renting a place just down the mountain," she told him. "It's a nice place, but it's not far from the home of one of Bitterwood P.D.'s finest."

"Aren't *you* one of Bitterwood P.D.'s finest?" He winced as she started down the winding mountain road, seeming to hit every bump and pothole along the way. The car fishtailed for a moment on the slick road, flinging him off the narrow seat onto the floorboard. He growled a couple of heartfelt profanities as pain knifed through his injured side.

"Damn, we got really close to a drop-off that time." Delilah's voice had a jittery, amped-up quality he remembered well. Brushes with death had always left her a little giddy, as if the mere act of surviving was a wellspring of joy. He'd wondered, more than once, if she carried that same reckless abandon with her into the bedroom.

And then, one snowy night in West Virginia, he'd learned the answer.

"How did you know I joined the Bitterwood P.D.?" she asked curiously. "I just made the decision a couple of weeks ago."

He didn't try to lie on the seat again, settling for a low slump against the back of the bucket seat on the driver's side. "Called Cooper Security and asked for you. Got a talkative receptionist."

"I'll have to mention that to Jesse," she murmured drily. But she didn't sound angry that he'd found her.

"Why'd you leave? I thought you were happy there."

Her eyes met his in the rearview mirror. "How would you know?"

"I assume you know by now that I've been in touch with Seth."

"Yeah, I know." In the mirror, her eyes narrowed. "Why's that?"

Because I wanted a connection to you, he thought. Aloud, he said, "I thought he'd be useful to the bureau. He had connections we could exploit. And when he went straight, he turned out to be a valuable asset."

"He said you put him in some dangerous situations, like in Bolen's Bluff. The Swains could have killed him if they'd ever found out he was working for the FBI."

"I didn't expect them to kidnap Isabel Cooper and put the whole damned mountain on red alert when she got away." Brand grimaced as they hit another pothole. "I haven't talked to him since I had to run. Did he figure out who was targeting Rachel Davenport?"

"It was her stepbrother," Delilah answered after a long

pause. "The police arrested him a couple of weeks ago, but he died in his cell. The autopsy was inconclusive."

"Cortland got to him."

"You make him sound like the bogeyman."

"He is, in all the ways that matter." Brand shifted position and regretted it immediately. "How much farther?"

"Almost there." Was that a hint of sympathy in her tone? He was beginning to wonder if she had any left for him. So far she'd seemed more cautious than worried.

"I didn't want to drag you into this mess."

"I was already in it."

They were off the mountain now, and the sleet had turned to rain, angling down from the sky in silver streaks reflecting the Camaro's headlights. The steady swish of the windshield wipers and the comforting warmth of the car's heater conspired to lull him to sleep, but he struggled to keep his eyes open.

They weren't safe yet.

She parked the Camaro in front of a small bungalow nestled in the woods on a dead-end road. The houses they'd passed moments earlier were no longer in view, leaving her house isolated from the rest of the world, surrounded by woods and mountains as far as the eye could see.

"Long way from Georgetown," he murmured.

She turned in the seat to look at him. "You have no idea."

He let her help him out of the car, forced to lean on her more than he'd anticipated. She wrapped her arm around his waist, careful not to touch his gunshot wound, and eased him up the shallow set of stairs to the wraparound porch.

"I'm sorry," he murmured when she settled him on a brown leather sofa in the front room.

"Don't apologize unless you draw blood," she muttered, parroting back a saying he'd taught her a long time ago.

She grimaced as she took a closer look at his bullet wound. "Gonna have an ugly scar."

"Won't be my first." He gritted his teeth as she plucked the fabric of his shirt away from the wound. "Got any pain-killers?"

"Just the over-the-counter type. Want a bullet to bite?"

"I see your bedside manner hasn't changed."

Her dark brows arched, and he realized with dismay the double-edged nature of his quip.

"This is going to hurt like hell." After digging in a nearby drawer, she returned with a soft-sided first-aid kit. "Be right back—I need more supplies."

She detoured long enough to lock the front door and disappeared into another room. Brand let his gaze drift across the front room, curious whether he'd be able to find anything he recognized of the woman he'd once believed could rise all the way to the top of the FBI.

There were few decorations—an empty umbrella stand near the door, an old Smoky Mountains tourist poster in a cheap metal frame hanging over the fireplace mantel. The sofa and a pair of matching leather armchairs looked comfortably broken in, but the plain oak coffee table between them looked new, chosen for utility over beauty. The floors were hardwood, softened by a brown woven rug that matched the sofas. The built-in bookcases on either side of the fireplace were only half-filled, mostly with thrillers, classics and nonfiction.

Delilah came back into the living room carrying a bucket full of soapy water and a handful of washcloths. "Sure you don't want that bullet to bite?"

"How long have you been living here?"

"Counting today? Two days."

That explained the scarcity of personal effects, he supposed. At least he hoped it did. Because right now, if he had

to profile her based on her home environment, he'd be leaning toward a diagnosis of antisocial personality disorder. And
that definitely wasn't the Delilah Hammond he remembered.

"You look good," he ventured as she sat on the coffee table
and dipped one of the washcloths into the bucket of suds.

One side of her mouth quirked. "Flattery won't make me
hurt you any less."

"I was just commenting."

She slanted a look at him. "You look like hell."

He laughed, stopping immediately when his injured muscles protested. "I still clean up pretty well, I promise."

Ten minutes of agony later, she smoothed down the last
strip of tape over his fresh bandage and sat back, looking at
him with dark, unfathomable eyes. "I hate to tell you this,
but I'll have to change that bandage first thing in the morning. But it won't take as long or hurt as much, I don't think."

"Why weren't you surprised?" He sounded weaker than
he expected, his voice thready and strained.

"By you showing up in the woods behind my mama's
house?"

He nodded.

"I've been waiting for you to show up here in Bitterwood
ever since I heard you went AWOL."

"How'd you know I'd come here?"

"The last case you were working started here. Where else
would you go?" She shrugged as if the answer was too obvious to require explanation. "I *am* a little curious about why
you went to my mama's house, though."

"That was the number the receptionist at Cooper Security gave me. She said you didn't have a home phone yet, but
you'd given them that number if anyone needed to contact
you. I got the address through the phone number."

"I see." A fleeting emotion glimmered in her eyes.

"You knew I'd call looking for you. Didn't you?"

She looked down at the bucket. "I'd better go get this cleaned up. You still hungry?"

The thought of food made him queasy. "I'm good for now. But you didn't get to eat, so you go ahead."

She disappeared from the living room for a few minutes, returning with a blanket and a pillow. "I have just the one bedroom, so it's up to you. You want to stay here on the sofa or try getting up and going to the bedroom?"

He was tempted to come back with a little teasing innuendo but quelled the urge. "I'm good here. Not in the mood for moving around at the moment."

"You didn't get a look at the person who shot you?"

"Blind ambush. I was too busy running for my life."

"So it might not have been this Cortland person."

"Oh, he wouldn't do his own dirty work. That's not his style."

She sat on the coffee table and leaned toward him, her elbows resting on her knees. She wasn't wearing a stitch of makeup, and she smelled like soapy water and disinfectant, but if he hadn't been laid up with a gunshot wound, he'd have done his damnedest to get back into her bed. Because she was still the most beautiful, exciting, interesting woman he knew.

Time apart hadn't done a damned thing to change that fact.

"Where did the shooting happen?" she asked.

"In Virginia. I'd stopped for coffee at a doughnut shop in Bristol. I came out of the shop heading for my car and got hit out of nowhere."

"You were in a car? Where is it now?"

"Parked it in a junkyard near Maryville. I've been on foot ever since."

She winced. "That's a long walk for an injured man."

"Tell me about it." Grimacing, he shifted on the sofa, trying to find a less painful position. She reached across and helped him fluff up the pillow under his head, her cool hand brushing across his face.

"You need antibiotics. We should get you to a real doctor."

"You know I can't go to a doctor."

"You were running around the woods with an open wound—"

"Guess we have to hope you cleaned it out sufficiently."

She fell silent for a moment. Then her gaze rose to meet his, her dark eyes troubled. "Why does the FBI think you're a traitor?"

"Because they have all sorts of damning evidence that suggests I am."

"Are you?"

Her flatly stated question felt like a punch in the gut. "I thought you said you already knew the answer to that question."

"Eight years is a long time. I'm not the same person. Maybe you're not, either."

He sat up to face her, ignoring the fire in his side. He caught her face between his palms, finding fierce satisfaction in the way her eyes dilated and her lips trembled apart. "You know me, Delilah. Better than anyone else in the world. That hasn't changed. It never will."

Her eyes fluttered closed, as if she couldn't bear what she saw in his gaze. He let her go, slumping back against the sofa cushions.

She stood and picked up the blanket she'd laid on the coffee table beside her. "Why don't you get some sleep? That'll do more to help you heal than anything."

He stretched out on his good side, watching her unfold the blanket with quick, efficient hands. "I'm sorry."

She shot him an exasperated look.

"I didn't know who else to come to."

Placing the blanket over him, she shook her head. "I

needed a spot of trouble in my life again," she murmured. "Things were threatening to get a little too tame around here, and you know how I hate that."

He closed his fingers over her wrist, holding her in place as she started to straighten. "I'm sorry about more than landing on your doorstep."

Her eyes darkened. "Yeah, me, too."

He let her go, and she gave the blanket a tug at the bottom, covering his feet.

"Hey, Brand?" she said.

"Yeah?"

"You could really use a bath and some deodorant."

He grinned at her as she started out of the room. "Duly noted."

She stopped in the doorway, turning back to face him. "Do you think Cortland knows where you are now?"

"I don't know," he admitted. "There's a lot I don't know."

She nodded, her jaw squaring, making her look more like the woman he remembered. "We'll have to assume he does."

"Then maybe I should go."

A familiar look of determination came over her face, sending a thrill through his aching body. Here was the Delilah Hammond he knew, he thought. Here was the woman who'd made his life an endless adventure. He hadn't realized until that very moment just how bloody empty his life had been without her.

"You're not going anywhere," she said firmly.

"He's not going to stop looking for me," Brand warned her.

Her chin lifted. "Let him come. We'll be ready."

Chapter Three

Snow had fallen in the mountains overnight, Delilah discovered when she wiped away the condensation on the kitchen windows the next morning. Peeking through the fog that gave the Smoky Mountain range its name, the firs and spruces in the higher elevations looked as if they'd been dusted with powdered sugar. Even here in the valley, a crust of hoarfrost covered the ground outside.

What would have happened to Adam Brand if she hadn't found him last night? Would he have survived the night at those temperatures? She tamped down a shudder at the thought and spooned coffee into the machine, making it extra strong, the way she liked it.

The way Brand liked it, too, she remembered. He was the one who'd taught her to like coffee in the first place. To this day, she still bought the brand of beans he liked, grinding them herself.

How much of who she was had been shaped by those years she'd worked at the FBI with Adam Brand?

Footfalls behind her made her jump. She turned to find Brand standing in the kitchen doorway, the blanket wrapped around his bare torso. His hair was mussed and there were dark circles of pain under his blue eyes, but there was no escaping the impact of his masculine presence. It tugged at her belly, impossible to ignore.

"I smelled coffee."

"You shouldn't be out of bed."

"I'm feeling better. You were right. Sleep helped."

She made herself look away from his bare chest, as broad and well toned as she remembered. Time hadn't robbed him of one ounce of virility. If anything, the lines of age now evident in his face only added to his masculine appeal.

He'd seen the difference in their ages as an obstacle. He'd never understood that she'd found his maturity one of his most tempting assets.

"You still put that flavored stuff in your coffee?" he asked when she opened the refrigerator and pulled out a bottle of hazelnut-flavored liquid creamer.

She made a face. "Do you still eat sardines?"

"Keeps me young."

She grabbed a couple of mugs from the cabinet next to the sink. "Black, no cream, no sugar?"

"Some things don't change."

She handed him a cup of steaming coffee. "Lots of things do, though."

He eased into one of the two chairs at a small table in her kitchen nook. "More things than not, I guess." He made a sound of satisfaction at the first sip of coffee. "None of the people who took your place could ever make coffee worth a damn."

"Nice to know I was irreplaceable in one aspect." She splashed creamer in her own coffee, added a packet of sweetener and carried the cup to the nook. She sat across from him, cocking her head to look him over. "You do look better this morning."

"Must be the company."

She stifled a smile. "Sweet talker."

"I'm serious. This is the first time since I went off the grid that I've felt any hope."

"How did this all happen?" she asked. "How did someone get close enough to frame you?"

Brand sighed, pushing his mug of coffee away from him. "That's a long story. And, as these things do, it started with a woman."

"HER NAME WAS Elizabeth Vaughn. U.S. Attorney out of Abingdon, Virginia. I met her at a University of Virginia alumni function, and it turned out we had a lot in common." Brand watched Delilah's face, trying to gauge her reaction. But her features were as inscrutable as a mask. "We started seeing each other whenever she was in D.C. on business. She's how I came to learn the name Wayne Cortland."

"It was one of her cases?"

"Peripherally. She'd been investigating militias in the Appalachians and discovered that most of them had connections to meth dealers in the area. And most of both groups—militia and drug dealers—had done business with Wayne Cortland at some point."

"So you think Cortland's part of the redneck mafia?"

"A little less redneck, a little more mafia. He actually runs a legitimate lumber mill in a town called Travisville, near the Virginia/Tennessee border."

"I've heard of Travisville," Delilah said. "They have a bluegrass festival. My father used to take us there. At least, that's why *we* went. *He* went to score drugs until he figured out how to make his own."

She always seemed so clinical when she talked about her father and his drug problems. Even when she'd described escaping the burning rubble of the house her father had blown up in a meth-cooking accident, she'd stuck to the facts, never talking about how she'd felt, at the tender age of seventeen, to lose her father and her home to his criminal stupidity.

How had she coped with her homelessness? With her injured brother and her drunk of a mother? How had she come through unscathed to earn a scholarship to a good college and forge a whole new life for herself?

Had she come through unscathed? He didn't see how it was possible. There had always been dark places in Delilah he'd never been able to reach.

Or maybe he just hadn't tried hard enough.

"Cortland's lumber business is legit," he said. "But Liz was sure he laundered drug money through it. She just hadn't figured a way to prove it."

"So she brought you in on it?"

"Peripherally. She suspected he might be funding some meth mechanics in the mountains who then funded the white-power militia groups that gave the meth dealers their own army. She wanted me to see if I could get the domestic-terrorism task force involved in trying to tie those militias—and the meth cookers—to Cortland and his business."

"Is he running the meth labs or just laundering the money?"

"I think he's running them. Liz and I were able to talk to a few people who'd defied Cortland. They live in terror because apparently Cortland's built this network of cookers and militia, and he keeps them in line with lethal threats. He's already shown he's willing to kill anyone who tries to cross him. We just can't come up with the proof, because even the people who dared to talk to us are too terrified to testify against him."

"Why didn't you go to Liz for help instead of coming here?"

"Liz is dead."

His flat pronouncement elicited the first emotion he'd seen out of Delilah—a visible recoil. "I'm sorry. Was it Cortland?"

"The FBI thinks it was me."

Her brow furrowed. "You? They think you killed some-one you were involved with? Why?"

"We weren't involved anymore. Not romantically." He shook his head, closing his fingers around the coffee mug to warm them. "The relationship never got very far—we were better suited as friends than lovers. But that didn't keep me from being the prime suspect when she was murdered. See, I was the one who found her."

"Oh, no."

"I was in Abingdon to meet with her about some new in-formation she'd gotten from an informant. When I got to her house, I found the door unlocked. She wasn't answering the door, so I let myself in."

"And you found her?"

He nodded, trying to put the scene out of his head. So much blood—

"You didn't have an alibi?"

"She was still alive. The shooting must have just hap-pened. I tried to stop the bleeding—" He swallowed hard, remembering the desperate fight to keep Liz alive. "There was just too much damage. But see, it had just happened. The timeline was too close. How could I prove I wasn't the one who'd done it?"

"Surely they checked you for gunshot residue. Checked your gun."

"She was shot with her own gun. And the killer wore gloves—they were lying next to the gun. No way to prove they didn't belong to me, although they can't prove they did, either."

"This is crazy."

"Tell me about it."

"All I heard was that you were suspected of espionage. Nobody talked about murder."

"The police haven't charged me with murder yet. Their focus was on what they'd found on Liz's computer."

Tension drew lines in Delilah's brow. "Which was what?"

"Emails from me, detailing our plan to frame Wayne Cortland for theft of nuclear material from the Oak Ridge National Laboratory."

Delilah sat back in her chair with a thump. "Emails from you?"

"Well, clearly, not from me. But whoever faked them knew what he was doing. I'd suspect me, too."

"Let me guess. Some of the militias had hooked up with anarchists?" Delilah didn't sound surprised. Maybe she'd come across something similar in some of her work with Cooper Security.

"We'd suspected all along that might be the case. When you're determined to bring down all civil government, you don't always care about the motives of your fellow travelers." Brand shook his head. "I thought I'd taken all the necessary precautions to protect myself from being targeted. I wasn't even working this case with Liz in an official capacity. But somehow Cortland figured it out."

"Liz must have known she was a target."

"Of course she did. She trusted the wrong person."

"You think someone betrayed her?"

"I know someone did. There was no sign of a struggle in her apartment. The alarm wasn't engaged. No sign of a break-in."

"So she let her killer into her apartment willingly."

Brand's side was beginning to ache. He tried to ignore the pain but he couldn't stop a grimace.

"I need to take a look at your wound." Delilah set her coffee to the side and stood up, holding her hand out to him.

He stared at her outstretched fingers, noting the short, neat nails and wondering if she still nibbled them when she was nervous. He put his hand in hers and it felt impossibly right. As always.

She helped him to his feet and looked at the bandage. "Not a lot of seepage through the bandage. That's good, I think."

"You hope," he murmured, not missing the uncertainty in her tone.

Her brown eyes met his. "You probably should have gone in search of a doctor for help. Might've been a little more pragmatic."

His fingers itched to touch her face, to trace the angular lines of her jaw and brush across her parted lips, but he balled his hands into fists and controlled the urge. "I just wish I hadn't put you right in the middle of all of this. You don't need the headache."

"What's one more headache?" Her lopsided half smile nearly shattered his control, and for a second he forgot the pain in his side, the trouble hanging over his head and the eight years that had passed since he'd last kissed Delilah Hammond's soft, pink mouth.

He wanted her. He'd wanted her from the first moment she walked into his office, all long legs and brilliant brains, and he had a feeling he was going to want her for the rest of his life.

What would she do if he told her she was the reason he'd never been able to take things to the next level with Liz? Or with any other woman he'd met since she walked into his office eleven years ago?

But he wouldn't tell her. Because one thing hadn't changed. He was still too wed to his job to be any good for a woman. Look how desperate he was to prove his innocence and get reinstated.

He'd already made the mistake of trying to have it all, and that had been a spectacular disaster. He wasn't going to make that mistake twice.

"There's some ibuprofen in the cabinet by the fridge. I'll go get the first-aid kit." She left the kitchen, giving him a chance to get his desire for her under control for the moment, though he was beginning to wonder how long he could ignore the truth.

All the other excuses—the proximity to Oak Ridge, the Davenport Trucking connection, his suspicion that Cortland might have allies in the small mountain town of Bitterwood— were meaningless in the face of his real reason for coming here.

He'd come to Tennessee because it was where she was. Even if there wasn't a damned thing he could offer her but more heartache.

She returned with the first-aid kit and the bucket of soapy water. "Want to do this here or in the living room?"

"Here is fine." He lifted his arm to give her easier access to his bandage. "Be careful. You know I'm delicate."

She slanted a look at him, as he'd intended. "Yeah, you're a real hothouse flower." Still, she was gentle as she tugged the tape away from the bandage she'd applied to his side the night before.

He sneaked a quick look at the furrow the bullet had torn in the skin just above his left hip. It appeared a bloody mess, but the margins of the wounds seemed less inflamed, as if healing had already begun. "What do you think?"

"It looks better. I wish I could get you some antibiotics, though."

"We'll keep an eye on my temperature and keep the wound clean. Maybe we'll get lucky."

Her gaze lifted to his. "I'm not a big fan of depending on luck."

He smiled. "Not everything can be planned to death, Hammond."

"Anything worth doing deserves the attempt to plan it to

death," she retorted, drenching a washcloth in the suds. She cleaned the wound as carefully as possible, wincing when he couldn't hold back a gasp of pain. "Sorry!"

"You should call your mother," he said as she patted the bullet wound dry and pulled out a tube of antibiotic cream. "So she doesn't come looking for you. You left there pretty quickly last night."

"I told her I had to help a friend in need."

"You have a lot of friends around here?"

She slanted a look up at him as she closed the tube. "Some."

"Any who'd be in enough trouble to drag you away from dinner with your mother?"

"Not really," she admitted. "But my mother doesn't know that."

He arched his eyebrows. His own mother had always known everything, even things he'd tried to keep secret from her. She'd been the one who'd first realized his feelings for the new female agent under his supervision weren't entirely professional. Even as she was fighting the cancer that finally took her, she'd seen past his casual remarks about his team and focused like a laser on his mentions of Delilah Hammond.

"You can't see her and stay her supervisor, you know," she'd told him. Brand was a third-generation FBI agent, so his mother knew the rules as well as he did, having been married to an agent for more than forty years. "You'll have to make a choice, just like before."

And he had, eventually. Just not the one Delilah might have wanted.

"Mothers know stuff," he warned Delilah as she applied a clean bandage to his injury. "Call her before she decides to drop by."

"I'll call her soon." Her fingers were warm and gentle,

making the flesh of his side ripple with awareness. He tried not to imagine her hands tracing a fiery path up his body, tried not to remember just how talented those hands could be when she chose to let them wander.

"How's she doing?"

Her answering look was wary. "She's gone on the wagon again."

"How long?"

"This is day four." She released a soft sigh. "She seemed to be doing well when I saw her last night. You don't think my leaving early would have set her off on a binge, do you?"

"I don't know," he admitted. During the handful of years he and Delilah had worked together, he'd seen her go through the hopeful highs and crushing lows of her mother's attempts at sobriety. "What do you think?"

"I think she's failed eight times before now. The odds aren't good."

And yet she still wanted to believe her mother could change. Hope, battered but not yet dead, hovered behind her dark eyes.

He cradled her face between his palms and pressed his lips to her forehead, helpless to stop himself. She stepped closer to him, her body brushing his. He felt the rapid thud of her heart against his chest, an echo of his own galloping pulse.

A pounding sound from the front of the house sent her skittering away, her face turning toward the sound. She uttered a low curse.

"Your mom?" he asked in a whisper.

"I don't know." She waved her arm toward the doorway. "My bedroom is the first room down the hall. Go there and lock the door. And take this stuff with you." She poured the water from the bucket into the sink, dropped the wet washcloth into it and shoved the bucket and the first-aid kit at him. While she grabbed the trash left over and threw it in the garbage can by the sink, he followed her directions and went to her bedroom, closing the door behind him and engaging the lock.

He put down the bucket and pressed his ear to the door, trying to hear what was going on at the front door. He heard the rattle of the dead bolt and the door swinging open with a creak.

"Oh. Hi." Delilah's voice, muffled by the closed bedroom door, sounded cautious. "What are you doing—?"

"Where is he, Delilah?" It was a male voice, hard and imperious.

Brand flattened his hand against the door, his heart suddenly in his throat. He looked around the room, at the lone, narrow window behind the bed, and felt like a trapped animal.

They knew he was here.

He'd done the one thing he'd most wanted to avoid, even though his instincts had driven him right to this little mountain town from the moment he'd first realized his life was in danger.

He'd brought that danger straight to Delilah Hammond's doorstep.

Chapter Four

"Hello to you, too, Antoine." Delilah forced herself to smile at her soon-to-be colleague, Detective Antoine Parsons of the Bitterwood Police Department. He was a tall, lean man in his early thirties, with smooth brown skin and coffee-dark eyes that had always been able to see through a load of bull at twenty paces, even back during their school days.

But how on earth could he know that Adam Brand was here?

Antoine met her smile with an arched eyebrow. "Where is Seth, Dee? I went by the Davenport place and it was locked up tight. Tried Cleve's old place and it's locked up, too."

She hid her relief. "I don't know. I haven't talked to him in a couple of days. I could call my mother and see if she's heard from him."

"We're trying to keep an eye on Rachel Davenport, damn it! Your brother is always pulling some stupid stunt that makes our jobs harder." Antoine sighed and looked at her disheveled state. "Did I wake you?"

"No, I've been up awhile." She pulled her robe more tightly around her, even though the thermal tee and sweats underneath weren't exactly revealing. "But I'm not interested in heating the outdoors this morning, so if you don't mind—"

She'd meant for him to leave, but he took her words as an invitation to enter, crowding past her into the living room.

If he'd been anyone else, she might have stood her ground and made him go, but Antoine was soon to be her colleague. She couldn't afford to alienate a potential ally before she'd even started her job.

"You don't think they've bugged out for good, do you?" Settling on the sofa, Antoine looked up at her, frustration shining in his eyes. "I'm getting all sorts of pressure from above as it is about not closing this case, and if he's just high-tailed it off—"

"You're getting pressure to close the case?"

He grimaced. "It's subtle, but yeah. Upper management would like to see it go away, now that the killer and the man who hired him are both dead."

"Somebody was twisting Bailey's arm to put out that hit," Delilah said flatly. "You know that as well as I do."

"Try proving it."

"A new lead would be nice." She sat in the armchair across from the sofa, trying not to think about the pillow she'd thrown hastily behind the sofa out of sight from the doorway. If Antoine decided he wanted a cup of coffee or something—

"The TBI says they're trying to track down the source of Bailey's gambling debts, but—"

But the Tennessee Bureau of Investigation had much bigger fish to fry than investigating a theory that someone had been pulling Paul Bailey's strings when he tried to drive his stepsister out of her role as CEO of Davenport Trucking. Rather than trying to figure out why control of the company might be worth killing people to get, the authorities seemed willing to write it off as one man's insane ambition.

Tension stretched through her body like a giant rubber band. She needed Antoine to go away. Now. "Well, I can tell you this. Wherever Seth is, he's with Rachel, and he'll take a bullet for her before he lets anything happen to her." She let her gaze drop, not wanting Antoine's sharp eyes to catch the fact that she was on edge.

That was when she spotted the torn gauze package.

Her nerve endings clanged as if someone had snapped that rubber band of tension. Balling her fists by her sides, she tried not to react, even though her pulse had jumped about twenty beats a minute.

The package must have fallen beneath the coffee table the night before when she was cleaning Brand's wound. It lay a few inches from Antoine's foot, just under the edge of the table, and it had a rusty splotch of dried blood on it. If he looked down at his feet—

She rose immediately. "Antoine, I don't mean to be rude, but I have some errands to run before lunchtime, and if I don't get to it—"

"Of course. Sorry." Antoine stood and shot her an apologetic smile. "If you hear from Seth or Rachel, will you let them know I'm trying to keep them, you know, alive?"

"Of course." She walked him to the door, keeping her body carefully between him and the coffee table.

He paused in the doorway, jangling her nerves again with his slow retreat. "I'm not quite sure why you decided to throw in your lot with us hicks here in Bitterwood, but I'm glad to have you on board. I've heard great things about you over the years. Your mother is very proud."

And very talkative when drunk, Delilah thought, immediately feeling disloyal. Her mother might not have a great track record at going off the booze, but last night she'd shown signs of really trying to get her life in order. Maybe she needed support, not more skepticism.

She'd give her a call just as soon as she got Antoine out of the way and Brand out of her bedroom.

"Thanks," she said to Antoine. "I'm actually looking forward to it." At least, she was looking forward to investigating a hunch she'd begun forming a few weeks earlier when she'd first come back to Bitterwood.

"Next Monday, right?"

She nodded. "That's right. Save a desk for me." She stood in the doorway until he drove away, then closed the door and sagged against it, her head pounding with delayed reaction.

"You can come out now," she called.

She heard the bedroom door creak open, and Brand came back into the living room, his brow creased. "Who was that?"

"Antoine Parsons, one of the Bitterwood cops. He's looking for Seth."

"Seth is missing?"

"*Missing* may be a strong word. My guess is, he got Rachel out of town for a while." She narrowed her eyes at Brand. "He didn't know you were in town, did he?"

Brand shook his head. "Nobody knows but you."

"We need to figure out what to do next."

"I've been thinking about that." He picked up the pillow she'd stashed behind the sofa and handed it to her, his expression somber. "I need to get out of here. All I'm doing is putting you in danger. Maybe it was just Antoine this time, but how long do you think it'll take for someone to figure out my connection to you?"

"I haven't worked for you in years."

"But your brother has. The FBI knows about it—they sanctioned his paychecks and took advantage of his information. And they know you and I were once on the same team."

She wondered, sometimes, if the FBI had ever suspected just how close she and Brand had come that one fateful night on an undercover assignment. She and Brand had barely spoken of it afterward, and within weeks she'd resigned from the FBI and left Washington behind.

Would his superiors think him likely to come here for help?

"I don't think anyone will connect us any time soon."

She tossed the pillow back on the sofa. "But it's probably a good idea if you take the bedroom from now on. Easier to hide evidence of your being here if you're not stuck in the front room."

"You're not listening to me." He put his hands on her arms, wincing a little as the movement apparently tugged his wound. "I have to go. I'm not going to put you in any more danger."

"You're not listening to *me*," she snapped back. "I'm not your underling, and you don't get to make this choice for me. You need help, and I intend to give it to you, at least until you're strong enough and well enough to have a chance in hell of surviving out there."

"If you're caught helping me, you'll be arrested."

The thought made her stomach ache. She'd spent most of her life priding herself on being the only Hammond from Bitterwood, Tennessee, who'd never stepped foot on the wrong side of a jail cell's bars.

"Yeah, think real hard about that, Hammond. I know what it would mean to you to be booked and incarcerated." His voice lowered, his head moving closer. "I'm not worth it."

Her gaze snapped up. "That's for me to decide. You came here for a reason. If it wasn't for me to help you, what was it?"

His eyes narrowed slightly, and he took a step back. "It wasn't for your help. At least not intentionally."

She felt a sinking sensation in her stomach. He'd always had a way of bursting her bubbles, hadn't he? "Then why?"

"A week before Liz died, she called me and mentioned that one of the private investigators she'd hired to follow Wayne Cortland had trailed him as far as Maryville. He said Cortland met a man in a coffee shop about three blocks from Davenport Trucking. He sent her a picture he'd snapped on his camera phone, but it wasn't the best resolution. He'd had to take it at a distance. But the photo seemed to show Cortland having coffee with Paul Bailey."

Delilah raised her eyebrows. "Why haven't we heard about this?"

"It was the last thing Liz heard from her P.I. The guy just disappeared off the map. Last I heard, nobody has a clue where he might be now."

"You think Cortland killed him?"

"Or had it done. Either way, I don't think the man's still alive. There's a whole lot of ways to disappear in these hills."

"Is anyone looking into his disappearance?"

"The Abingdon cops opened a case, but there aren't any leads to follow. Maryville can't even find record the guy was in town, except for that photo he sent. There's nowhere to look."

"You think this is evidence Cortland was manipulating Bailey into driving Rachel out of Davenport Trucking's CEO position?"

"If Cortland's pulling the strings on an Appalachian drug organization, I'm sure he'd find it helpful to have a whole fleet of trucks at his disposal. What if the debt Bailey owed was to Cortland? It would give Cortland a lot of leverage."

Delilah's head was beginning to ache again. She put her hand on Brand's arm, closing her fingers around the hard muscles when he flinched as if he was ready to pull away. "I know I can't stop you if you want to leave. But I also can't ignore the things you've told me. I'm starting work with the police department next week, and I'm going to want to follow these leads. If you're right, a man's been murdered right here in my neck of the woods. And there's another man plotting God only knows what that could affect the people I'll be paid to protect and serve. So if you think you'll be sparing me any grief, you won't. You'll just be leaving me without backup and important information I'll probably need to know."

He clapped his hand over hers where it lay on his forearm. "I don't want any of this to touch you."

She pressed her lips into a thin line, both moved and frustrated by his inclination to shield her. "I'm not fragile and I'm not helpless. I need your trust and respect, not your protection."

"You know you have that." He sounded offended.

She shook her head. "If you trusted and respected me, you wouldn't be trying to control what I do. You did this same thing before, Brand. You made decisions for me, to hell with what I thought or wanted. You always think you know what's best for other people."

He looked down at her hand. "Right now, I don't know what's best for anyone. Including myself. It's all gone so wrong, and I don't have a clue how to fix it."

She loosened her grip on his arm, her frustration fading. For all his exasperating, control-freakish ways, he still had a good heart. She'd questioned his actions many times over the years they'd worked together, but never his motives.

"That's what I'm for." She let go of his arm and nodded her aching head toward the kitchen. "Let's find something to eat. Problems always look a little less awful on a full stomach."

He looked at her for a long moment, as if teetering on the edge of an important decision. Finally, he gave a nod and followed her into the kitchen.

She released a silent breath, relieved. She had a feeling if he was right about his theories—and so far they were meshing all too well with what she knew about the Davenport Trucking conspiracy case—he might be the key to breaking this whole thing open and flushing out the bad guys she knew were still hiding in the shadows, waiting for the investigation to die down.

She didn't intend to let anyone get away with murder in her hometown.

LIGHT SNOW FLURRIES floated down from the glassy sky, swirling in the wind and melting as soon as they touched the ground. Not cold enough to stick, Brand thought as he gazed through the narrow gap in the front-room curtains.

"Still snowing?" Delilah's warm drawl sent a flush of masculine awareness sizzling up his spine. Her voice had been his first introduction to her, with its sultry timbre wrapped around a faint mountain twang. She'd answered his call to the Baltimore field office and he'd realized in an instant that he needed her on his team.

He'd thought it would be a temporary assignment, as he and the domestic-terrorism task force were heading to the mountains of North Carolina on a manhunt. He could tell she was from the general area, and she probably knew more about getting in and out of the small mountain towns without raising alarms than anyone else on his task force did.

He'd been right, although it hadn't taken long once he set eyes on her to realize she was nothing but trouble, and mostly to him.

"Just flurries," he answered her question. "What's the weatherman saying?"

"Snow in the hills again tonight." She had showered and changed into a pair of jeans that did wonderful things for her legs and backside and a long-sleeved heather-gray T-shirt that did wonderful things to the rest of her. He couldn't hold back a smile, drawing a quirk of her eyebrows.

"What?"

"Just remembering the first time I laid eyes on you in that cherry-red suit with the skirt about two inches shorter than every other woman's in the bureau. You walked in there determined to make an impression, and you did. I had to slap every man on the task force upside the head to get their eyes back in their skulls."

"*You* weren't impressed."

"I just didn't show it."

"I think I'd probably do things differently now." She crossed to stand by him at the window, gazing out at the front yard. Flurries were beginning to linger on the fallen leaves in the yard, melting more slowly. She rubbed her arms briskly. "Temperature's dropping. We may get some of that accumulation here as well."

"Will it snow us in?" he asked, trying not to wish for it. He had so much to do and time was running out. The last thing he could let himself do was lose focus because of Delilah.

But that was the effect she'd always had on him, wasn't it?

"No, the road surfaces are still too warm. But it's coming." She looked up at him. "Are you going to keep fighting me on this? Or are you going to let me help you?"

"You start a new job soon, don't you?"

"On Monday."

So, a week. How much could he get done in a week, even with her help? He and Liz had been looking into Cortland's business, albeit unofficially, for over a month, and they'd gotten almost nowhere.

Almost.

But Liz, as sweet and smart as she'd been, wasn't Delilah Hammond. Liz had been a city girl from Ohio trying to navigate a region that might as well have been another country.

Delilah had grown up in these hills. She knew their dark side, knew how to make her way through them, how to speak the language and carry herself so that she blended in rather than stuck out.

He was going to have to depend on those skills again. Like it or not.

"Okay. We'll work on this for the next week. But if we get nowhere, I've got to get out of here and let you get on with your life. Agreed?"

Her eyes narrowed, but she finally nodded. "Agreed."

He didn't know whether he felt relief or dread. A week with Delilah seemed like an unearned gift in so many ways. But was he just setting himself up for another round of regrets?

He had a bad habit of wanting things he could never let himself have.

Chapter Five

When Brand returned from taking a shower, his face looked pinched and pale. Delilah winced as he crossed to where she sat at the kitchen table making notes. "You okay?"

He nodded. "The wound hurts like hell, but I'm not seeing signs of infection." He turned his side to her for inspection.

He was right. The bullet groove seemed to be healing already, the ragged edges of flesh starting to look less angry and red. She took the digital temporal thermometer from the first-aid kit and handed it to him. "Take your temperature while I replace the bandage."

"Ninety-nine point two," he said a few seconds later as she placed a padded bandage over the bullet furrow.

"Not bad," she said. "If it goes over a hundred, we'll start worrying."

He waited for her to tape down the bandage. "We need to discuss the matter of clothes."

She looked up at him, her lips curving. "I don't know, Brand. I kind of like you walkin' around my house half-naked. Like I finally got that cabana boy I've always wanted."

He made a face at her. "It's a little chilly to play cabana boy. As fun as that sounds."

She felt a blush rising up her neck, reminding her she was a lot better at talking a good game than actually playing it. After she'd left Bitterwood to go to college on a scholarship and what money she could make from part-time jobs, she'd learned that scared little girls from the sticks always ended up crushed and forgotten in the big city. So she'd put on the sassiest, brassiest persona she could come up with and discovered she could go anywhere she wanted and do anything she wanted and nobody gave her any trouble.

Of course, it hadn't made her very popular with other women, and honest relationships with men had proved pretty damned hard to come by. But she couldn't help what women thought, and she didn't care what men thought, because the last thing she'd wanted, after growing up in the house with Delbert and Reesa Hammond, was a long-term relationship with a man.

Nobody was going to have that kind of control over her life, she'd vowed. She would *never* become what her mother had become.

Only Adam Brand had ever tempted her to think twice about happily ever after. And that hadn't exactly turned out well.

"What did you do with the clothes you had with you?" she asked, patting down the last piece of surgical tape. "Or did you run away from home with just the clothes on your back?"

He sat in the chair next to her. "There are some things in a canvas duffel bag stashed near a big truss bridge that goes over a gorge. Close to some seedy little bar out in the middle of nowhere."

"Purgatory Bridge," she murmured, wondering if he knew how that bridge had figured into her brother's life recently. Seth had saved Rachel Davenport's life on that bridge less than a month ago, and now they were already talking rings and forever. "I can get it for you now if you can describe where you left it."

"I'd probably have to be there." He glanced at the papers spread out in front of her. "What's all this?"

"My notes on the Davenport Trucking case," she answered. "I was just adding the things we discussed about Wayne Cortland."

He picked up the notes and glanced over them. "Thorough, Hammond. Guess I taught you a few things after all."

"A few," she conceded, dragging her gaze away from the muscular curve of his shoulder. "You sure you have to be there for me to fetch your clothes?"

"I hid the bag well. It would be easier for me to find it myself."

"It's cold out, and you're half-naked."

He shot her a grin. "Does that bother you?"

"That it's cold out?"

"That I'm half-naked."

"No," she lied.

He just kept grinning.

"In this weather, it'll be dark enough by five-thirty to risk it," she said. "I can't go out with a strange man in daylight around here. People would notice."

"I never thought I'd see you back here. You used to talk about this place as if it was hell. What did you call it—the Smoky Ridge curse?"

"Yeah. The Smoky Ridge curse. People who made it off Smoky Ridge always brought a little bit of hell with them. You can ask Seth about that sometime."

"I have. He agrees, and yet he's back here again, too."

She shrugged. "Can't escape it, so you might as well come back and face it, I guess. Another old friend of ours from childhood came back here to stay recently, too."

"Sutton Calhoun, right?"

She nodded. "His daddy's the one who got Seth into the con game. I never figured Sutton would step foot in this town again, but here he is."

"Seth says Calhoun's involved with one of the local cops?"

"Right. Ivy Hawkins. I'll be working with her at the police station."

"Two female detectives on a force this size in a place this small?"

She shrugged. "Maybe they're trying to meet a quota. I don't care why. I know I can do the job, and I'm glad to have it."

"I could get you back on the domestic-terrorism task force—" Brand stopped short, his smile fading. "Well, I could have."

Impulsively, she reached across the table and covered his hand. "We're going to get you back there again."

He turned his hand over, palm up, and closed his fingers around hers. His hand was hot, the skin of his palm a little rough, reminding her that he'd always been a man who liked working with his hands, even when he was stuck behind a desk. He'd worked with wood, building things like cabinets, tables and, once, for her birthday, a remarkably intricate teakwood jewelry box. She still had it, sitting in a storage unit back in Maybridge, where she'd put most of the stuff from her apartment before moving into this rental house in Bitterwood.

She wondered if she'd left so many things back in Alabama as a safety net, in case coming back here to Bitterwood didn't work out.

"What are you thinking?" he asked in a half whisper that sent a delicious shiver up her spine. She'd always liked his voice, the deep timbre and the leftover hint of coastal Georgia that his years in D.C. hadn't been able to obliterate.

"Just wondering if you still do that woodworking you used to do."

"Not at the moment," he said with a lopsided quirk of his mouth. His voice lowered a notch. "But you don't forget how to work with your hands."

Another tremor of sexual awareness rocketed through her, transporting her mind back eight years to a night in a tiny mountain bed-and-breakfast in West Virginia. It had been snowy that night, too, and their case had ended that afternoon with a successful arrest. The storm had delayed their flight, forcing them to stay one more night at the inn.

What happened that night had changed her life in so many ways.

She pulled her hand from his and rose, pacing away from the table. "I need to call my mother, see how she's getting on. Why don't you go look through my closet? I may have some oversize sweatshirts in there."

He stood, cocking his head thoughtfully. "Leftovers from old boyfriends?"

"Leftovers," she said simply, leaving it at that.

He took a deep, sharp breath through his nose and walked past her out of the kitchen, his shoulder brushing against hers.

She let out a breath and pressed her head against the kitchen wall, hating how rattled and on edge she felt when he was around.

Hating it—and craving it.

PURGATORY BRIDGE, STANDING thirty feet above Bitterwood Creek, was one of the only remaining truss bridges in the county, and it had seen better days even when Delilah had been a child, crossing it daily on her walk from Smoky Ridge to school. She'd walked across the span more times than she could remember, but she still felt a little flutter in her belly as the Camaro hit the bridge, wondering if this would be the time the whole thing would come crashing down into the gorge.

But they made it safely across, and Brand said, "It's just over there." He waved his hand toward a narrow path leading into the woods from the road, and Delilah parked the

Camaro well off the road, mindful of the bright neon lights of Smoky Joe's Tavern about fifty yards down Old Purgatory Road. Even on a Monday night, the bar's parking lot was nearly full, and anyone could drive by at any time, spot the Camaro and stop to see what was going on.

"We need to hurry," she whispered as she followed him into the woods.

"It's near a fallen tree." His eyes narrowed as he peered into the gloom. "It was right over—" He pitched forward suddenly and fell to the ground.

"Brand!" Barely avoiding tripping over him, Delilah crouched beside him as he tried to regain his feet. He groaned as her hand brushed against his injured side. "Sorry!"

"I'm okay." He didn't sound okay, his voice reedy with pain. "Foot caught on a tree root."

She helped him dust off, looking around in the dark woods for the fallen tree he'd mentioned. A little moonlight would have helped her see through the dark, but the weatherman was promising another chance of snow, this time in the lower elevations as well, and a thick layer of heavy clouds blotted out any light from the heavens. Only the garish reflected glow of the bar down the road gave them any illumination at all.

"There," Brand said, waving his arm toward a black mass barely distinguishable from the rest of the shadows in the thick woods. He bent at his waist, still trying to catch the breath his fall had knocked from him, so she moved toward the dark shape, relieved when her eyes adjusted enough to recognize that it was, indeed, a fallen tree.

She found the duffel bag tucked up under the tree trunk where the snapped section was still connected to the rooted stump. It was water-resistant vinyl and seemed to have come through the previous night's storm without much damage.

They hurried back to the edge of the woods, waiting for headlights to pass before risking a quick dash to the Camaro.

Delilah threw the duffel into the backseat and cranked the car, a bubble of laughter escaping her throat. "Just like old times."

She felt Brand's gaze like a touch, but she didn't let herself turn to look at him, easing the Camaro back onto Old Purgatory Road, headed toward Smoky Ridge.

"When you talked to your mother this afternoon, did you ask if she'd heard anything from Seth?" Brand asked a few minutes later, after Delilah had begun to relax, certain no one was following them.

"He and Rachel spent the night in Bryson City, North Carolina. Rachel's uncle has a music hall there. Mama said they're probably driving back tonight."

"Was she curious about why you left so suddenly last night?"

"A little. I think I reassured her nothing's wrong."

His next question came out in a careful tone. "How was she?"

"You mean, was she drunk?"

He didn't answer.

"She was sober when I talked to her."

"Maybe it'll last this time." He didn't sound hopeful, she noticed.

Couldn't really blame him for that. He'd been by Delilah's side through a couple of her mother's attempts at sobriety several years ago. He'd seen her hopes dashed both times.

"Maybe it will," she agreed. She didn't sound very hopeful, either.

They built a fire in the fireplace when they got back to her house, pulling the leather armchairs close enough to warm themselves against the descending chill of night. Outside, snow flurries had begun to fall, fluttering against the windows in a hushed whisper.

Delilah noticed he was favoring his side as he sat. She

crouched in front of him, looking up into his pain-lined face. "Did you reinjure yourself when you fell?"

He grimaced as she reached for the hem of his sweatshirt. "Probably just a bruise."

She pulled up his shirt and examined the area around his bandage. She didn't see any blood peeking through the gauze, but there was an area of skin around the bottom of his rib cage that was beginning to grow purple. "Yeah, a nasty bruise. Does it hurt when you take a breath?"

He tested his ribs with a deep breath. "Not particularly."

She pressed her fingertips against the bruised area, checking for any sign of instability in the rib cage. It felt normal enough. "Probably didn't crack a rib, then."

She looked up and found Brand's face close to hers, his blue eyes dark and intense. "Remember Pike City?" His voice was a faint rasp.

She nodded, her heart thudding. "Those hillbillies beat the hell out of you. I was afraid I wasn't going to get you out of there alive."

"First time you played nurse for me." His mouth curved, a flash of white teeth peeking between his lips. "I couldn't tell you how damned sexy you were, trussing me up and getting me back on my feet so we could get out of Kentucky alive."

She arched an eyebrow, trying to pretend his words didn't send a shiver of desire skittering through her. "Sexy? I was scared to death."

"But you didn't show it. You were so fierce."

She started to stand, but Brand caught her wrist, holding her in place. She closed her eyes, trying to fight the tremors his touch elicited. "Brand, please—"

"Did you think of me after you left?" His words rumbled through her. "Did you think of me at all?"

She snapped her eyes open, wanting him and hating him

all at once. "For a long time, you were almost all I thought about."

His eyes flickering with an emotion she couldn't quite discern, he released her wrist and looked away. "I'm sorry."

She pushed to her feet and backed away, sitting in the other armchair. She turned her gaze to the fire, trying to control the reckless emotions darting through her. She didn't make decisions based on her feelings. She'd made that mistake once, in a snowy mountain inn in West Virginia.

She didn't think she could survive making the same mistake twice.

For a long time, the crackle of the fire and the soft whisper of snow against the windows were the only sounds in the room, and if she hadn't been one raw nerve, Delilah might have dozed off.

But there was no way to relax with Brand in the room. With him around she felt edgy and vulnerable, fire licking her belly and fear squeezing her heart. No one had ever gotten beneath her skin the way Adam Brand had. No one had made her feel so unraveled, so alive, so vulnerable.

And the worst part was, as much as she hated the feeling of walking on a high wire with no net below her, she found it equally exhilarating.

It had been a long time since she'd felt this reckless and on fire.

Eight years, to be exact.

"I should go change into the clothes we brought back," Brand said a few minutes later, breaking the taut silence. He rose carefully from the chair. "These jeans are getting kind of ripe."

"How long have you been running?" she asked as he reached the doorway.

He turned, giving her one of those long, electric looks she used to crave. "Feels like eight years," he murmured.

Then he disappeared through the doorway.

DRESSING BY HIMSELF was proving a painful experience, and the temptation to call Delilah into the bedroom to help him was almost more than Brand could resist. But the phone had rung a couple of minutes earlier, and he could still hear the soft murmur of Delilah's voice as she spoke to whoever was on the line.

He zipped the clean pair of jeans and went back to the living room, taking care to be quiet. Delilah was curled up in her chair, her long legs tucked under her, listening to whoever was on the other end of the call.

"Are you sure it was just a careless driver?" She glanced up at Brand as he took the chair next to her, her brow furrowed. "I don't know, Seth. The timing sounds pretty hinky."

Brand leaned forward, not liking the sound of her end of the conversation.

"Just call me when you're safely home, okay? Talk to you soon." She ended the call and laid the phone on the arm of the chair. "Seth and Rachel were nearly run off the road driving home from North Carolina."

"Are they okay?"

"Yes, but they're still about an hour away. They stopped at a scenic overpass where there were a few more people parked. Safety in numbers." Delilah still looked worried.

"What do you want to do?" he asked quietly.

Her dark eyes met his. "I want to go run interference for them."

"Where are they?"

"A few miles over the North Carolina state line."

Going out again would be a risk. Any time he might be spotted in public was a risk. And while he was pretty sure

Seth Hammond wouldn't turn him in to the authorities, he didn't know enough about Rachel Davenport to know whether he could trust her to do the same. Either way, he'd be asking them to break the law in order to protect him, a situation that went against everything he'd ever believed.

How had he allowed Cortland to put him in this position?

"I know you don't want to bring Seth into this," Delilah said.

He saw understanding in her dark eyes, a reminder of just how naked she could make him feel sometimes. She knew him about as well as he'd ever allowed anyone to know him. When they'd worked together, it had helped them create a sort of efficient shorthand, a minimal need for words that had come in handy in more than one high-risk situation.

Her perception had also damned near unraveled him.

The phone rang again, rattling his nerves. Delilah grabbed it, checked the display and answered. "Seth?"

Brand heard the buzz of Seth Hammond's voice coming over the line, his tone quick and agitated. He leaned forward, worried by the darkening look on Delilah's face.

"Are you sure they're following—?"

A loud sound cracked through the receiver, audible even where Brand sat. He rose to his feet, instantly on alert.

"Seth!" Delilah exclaimed. "Seth?" She repeated her brother's name a couple times more, then punched a button. "The line went dead," she growled, pushing in a phone number. After a moment, she snapped the end button with a jab of her thumb, growling a curse.

"Was that—?"

"A gunshot?" She nodded, already grabbing her jacket from the back of the sofa, her face pale and pinched. "Yes, it was."

He knew all the perfectly logical reasons he should stay put, safe from discovery. But Delilah's brother wouldn't have been in any of this trouble if Brand hadn't pushed him into the Davenport Trucking investigation.

He'd be damned if he'd leave a man in trouble to fend for himself, whatever the consequences.

Chapter Six

The phone call came about twenty minutes into Delilah's gut-wrenching drive down Little River Road, a dark and twisty mountain road with few turnoffs and almost no way to escape someone intent on doing a person harm. She grabbed the cell phone and punched it on Speaker. "Seth?"

"We're okay," Seth said quickly, sounding breathless. Delilah felt more than heard Brand's faint exhale of relief in the seat next to her. "But we're hiding down a dead-end road. So far, we think the guys who shot at us didn't backtrack to look for us, but once they figure out we're not ahead of them—"

"Which road?"

"It's just off the big switchback that crosses Little Pigeon River. We're off the road, in case they come back, but there's no good place to hide the car back here. We're out in the woods right now."

"In the snow?"

"Yeah, in the snow," Seth answered flatly. "And it's cold as hell. How far out are you?"

"Fifteen minutes. Ten if I push it."

"Push it," Seth said tersely.

"Ask about the vehicle," Brand whispered, barely audible even in the close confines of the Camaro.

"Seth, did you get a look at the vehicle that ambushed you?"

"Black Ram truck, one of those big extended-cab jobs with the double tires on the back."

"Ram 3500," Rachel's voice interjected. She sounded cold and scared.

"Got it," Delilah said. "I'm nearly there, Seth. Y'all just hold on."

"Will do." He hung up.

Brand pushed the off button on the phone for her. "You watch the road. I'll watch for that truck."

The snow was starting to stick, making for a slick and terrifying drive through the mountain passes. More than once the Camaro started to fishtail, but she kept it on the road, drawing on the driving skills she'd learned at Cooper Security. God bless Jesse Cooper and his obsession with training his agents for any eventuality.

About ten minutes later, Brand asked, "How far are we from the turnoff?"

She peered ahead, trying to remember. She'd traveled this road into the mountains hundreds of times in her childhood and teenage years. The big loop in the road was just ahead, and the river crossing wasn't far after that. "We're about two minutes away."

"So why haven't we seen the truck?"

Brand's question sent ice skating down her spine. "Maybe we passed it farther back, before we talked to Seth?"

"Maybe." Brand sounded doubtful.

He was right. The truck wouldn't have reached them by the time Seth called. But they should have passed it by now.

"They've doubled back to look for them," Delilah growled.

Brand reached into his jacket and pulled out a gleaming black Ruger SR9, his weapon of choice. Her own Sig was tucked behind her back in the pancake holster. When the road straightened out for a few dozen yards, she drew the P229. She held it out to Brand. "Check the mag."

He confirmed the pistol had ten rounds in the magazine and one in the chamber. "Locked and loaded." He held on to the Sig. "You drive. I'll hold the weapons."

They rounded a curve and the turnoff came into view. The road was paved but little more than that, disappearing into the woods. Delilah pulled the Camaro into the turn, her headlights splashing across the snowy woods.

At the end of the road, taillights glowed red in the winter gloom.

"That's a dually truck," Brand said.

She nodded. "What do we do? Try to draw their attention to us?"

"If it's Cortland's people, they may not even know what I look like," Brand answered. "If Liz was right about how he did business—and everything I know about him supports her theory—he runs his underlings in tight, self-contained cells. He's the only one who knows who all the players are—the people in each cell know only each other and any breach of security within the cell will earn them instant, brutal punishment. It doesn't take much to merit the death penalty in Cortland's organization."

"So this pair in the truck may know only about Seth and Rachel?"

"They'd know as much as they needed to know and no more. Fewer chances of an operational breach."

"So for all they know, we might be a pair of horny lovers looking for a snowy place to get our freak on?" Delilah asked with a huff of grim laughter.

"We've played that role before, sugar," he answered in a gravelly drawl that made her insides squirm. "What's the layout ahead?"

"The road ends right at the edge of the woods, in a circle. There's room enough for about three or four vehicles to park there. It's a sort of mountain make-out spot, though not usually in this kind of weather." She eased the Camaro down the road, pulling close enough to the truck to confirm it was a black Ram 3500 with dual wheels on the back.

"That's our truck," Brand said.

"And that's Seth's Charger." Delilah slipped the Camaro into an empty place behind the Charger. The truck hadn't moved, idling in the middle of the circle with its bright lights shining on the side of the Charger. There were a couple of bullet holes visible in the side panel over the right rear tire, she saw, swallowing a rush of anxiety. There was also a spiderweb of cracked glass in the back window where another bullet had hit.

"Close call," Brand murmured, turning to look at her. "Operation Snuggle?"

She bit back a bark of nervous laughter. "I could still kill you for that moniker." Nevertheless, she crawled over the gearshift and into his lap, trying hard not to look out the window toward the idling truck.

She felt the cold steel of his Ruger where his hand rested against the small of her back. She curled her hand over her own weapon, taking it from his left hand. Keeping the pistol carefully concealed by the side of the bucket seat, she pressed her forehead to his. "Do you think they'll shoot at us anyway?"

His breath was warm against her chin. "I hope to hell not."

She was too scared to feel anything but terror, a lesson she'd learned years earlier on her first "Operation Snuggle," as Brand jokingly called any undercover session requiring the agents to pretend to be lovers. Even the times she'd had to pretend with Brand, to whom she was wildly attracted under most circumstances, her body didn't have the capacity to feel anything but a wild rush of adrenaline.

It was afterward, when the danger had passed and the adrenaline faded, that hormones took over.

But even now, with the knowledge that the truck growling beside them contained at least one armed and dangerous person, Delilah was surprised to feel a flicker of sexual hunger low in her belly. A reminder, perhaps, of just how long it had been since she'd touched Brand this way.

Brand's left hand, now pistol free, slid under the hem of her jacket and crept beneath her thermal sweater until his cool fingers played over the hot skin of her waist. "Kiss me."

She lowered her mouth to his slowly, her heart pounding. His lips were warm and dry, soft at first, but hardening as her mouth met his. She threaded her fingers through his dark hair, slanting his head so that their mouths fit together more completely.

Kissing him still felt like sin and salvation, contradictory and irresistible. She knew she couldn't let herself want him, but she was powerless to resist the pull of attraction. Nothing— not their present danger or their past betrayals—could stem the tide of her desire.

The sound of the truck shifting gears dragged her back to reality. She pulled away from the kiss and slanted a sideways look out the window. The truck was backing out of the cul-de-sac.

Bending to press a kiss to Brand's forehead, she kept her eyes on the truck's headlights as it pulled a three-point turn and headed back toward the highway, its taillights filling the Camaro's interior with a bloodred glow. The glow faded as the truck disappeared around a bend in the road, out of sight. Delilah dropped her forehead against Brand's.

"They could be waiting to ambush us on the way out," Brand warned.

"I know." She didn't move out of his lap, giving herself permission to enjoy the feel of his body beneath hers for a few moments longer.

"I think we wait about five minutes before contacting your brother."

She pasted a sly smile on her face, even though her heart was still pounding from the adrenaline rush. "You want to wait in this position?"

His blue eyes glittered up at hers in the glow of the dashboard lights. "Is that a serious question?"

She shook her head, settling herself more firmly in his lap. "No."

His hand had never ceased doing shivery things to the skin of her back. "I never could resist you when you were in a flirty mood."

"Bull. You resisted the hell out of me for years. I know, because I think I spent the first three years of my assignment to your team trying to get you to look at me as something besides that smart-mouthed rookie agent you had to put up with."

His voice lowered to a growl. "I wanted to throw you across my desk about two seconds after you walked into my office that first day, Hammond."

Heat flooded her insides. "What a coincidence. I wanted the same thing."

Smiling, he shook his head. "An old, stuffy guy like me?"

"You were thirty-four. Hardly geriatric."

"Old enough. You were still a kid."

"I hadn't been a kid since I was fourteen years old and my daddy tried to trade me to a pseudoephedrine dealer to get supplies for his meth lab."

Brand froze. "You never told me about that."

She shook her head, wishing she hadn't brought it up. "There's a lot I never told you about."

"What did you do?"

"I got my daddy's shotgun and threatened to kill them both if either one of them touched me."

He flattened his hand against her back. "I just bet you did."

"There's not a lot I'm scared of anymore," she said quietly. "Once you've faced down things like that—"

He wrapped his hand around the back of her neck and drew her close, pressing a kiss to her forehead.

"How much time has passed since the truck left?" she asked, drawing away when she felt tears stinging her eyes. She blinked them away.

"Five minutes," he answered with a glance at the dashboard display.

She sat back on his knees, reached for her cell phone in the dashboard holder and dialed her brother's number.

He answered on the first ring. "Please tell me that was the truck we heard leaving, not you."

"That was the truck you heard leaving," she answered. "But I can't be sure they're not lying in wait closer to the highway."

"I'm not sure we can drive out of here. I thought one of the rounds might have hit the left rear tire. Can you tell from where you are?"

She twisted around to get a look at the back of the Charger. "I can't really see the tire from where I am, but the car does seem to be listing toward that side."

Seth muttered a profanity. "I'm going to have to take the backseat of that stupid sardine can of yours, aren't I?"

"Afraid so," she answered. "I'm parked right behind the Charger. Hurry, but try to keep a low profile, in case anyone's watching."

She hung up the phone and stretched across the gear column to unlock the driver's door.

"This is how you want your brother to find us?" Brand asked drily.

"He'll be shocked either way," she answered. "And this

way, I don't have to get out to move the seat forward so they can get in."

Two jacket-clad figures glided out of the woods, staying low but moving at a clip toward the Camaro. Seth reached the car first and gave a quick knock on the window before opening the door.

He bent and looked inside, freezing as he locked gazes with Delilah. His mouth dropped open.

"Get in, and hurry," she commanded. "I'll explain once we're all safely locked in."

Seth swallowed whatever questions he had and pushed the driver's seat forward, backing away to let Rachel climb into the backseat. Rachel's blue eyes widened at the sight of Delilah straddling a stranger's lap, but she slid across to the far side of the narrow seat, giving Seth room to climb in behind her.

"I can explain," Delilah murmured with a sly grin at her brother.

"Does it require me to kick his ass?"

"No," she answered, wriggling back across the gearshift and sliding into the driver's seat. "Rachel Davenport, this is Adam Brand."

In the rearview mirror, Rachel's mouth formed an O, but she managed to recover quickly, murmuring, "I've heard a lot about you."

Brand slanted a look at Delilah. "I'm sure you have."

"I know there's not much room, but I need you both to get down as far as you can. Make yourselves invisible. If they're waiting in ambush, they may not bother us if they think it's just Brand and me."

She waited until she could no longer see her brother or Rachel in the rearview mirror before she started the car. Easing around the circle, she headed back out the way she'd come, toward the highway.

Her heart skipped a beat as they rounded the curve and saw the red taillights of the Ram 3500, parked on the right side of the road, just off the pavement.

"They're going to have a good look inside," Delilah warned. "Stay very, very still and quiet."

Brand turned in his seat toward her, placing the back of his head toward the window. No one in the truck would be able to get a good look at him. He showed Delilah his Ruger. She waved the Sig in her right hand at him, then lowered it to the gearshift, hiding it from view.

She took care not to slow her speed as she passed the truck, allowing herself only the slightest of sidelong glances toward the vehicle, enough to see that mud caked the license plate, obscuring most of the letters and numbers from easy view. The truck's windows were closed, their dark tinting hiding the occupants.

She pulled to a stop at the T-intersection with the highway. Seeing no traffic approaching from either direction, she eased onto the highway and headed east, away from Bitterwood and toward the North Carolina state line. She waited another couple of minutes before she spoke. "They didn't follow us. You can get up now."

She kept her eye on the road, which had become even more slippery since she'd made the detour down the side road. Snow was falling in fat clumps now, forcing her to turn on the windshield wipers.

"We're not going back to Bitterwood?" Seth asked from the backseat.

"I'm not sure," she answered. "I just know we can't go back the way we came. If that truck's still sitting there watching and they spot us coming back, they might get a little curious as to why."

"We can go back to Bryson City," Rachel suggested. "My uncle could probably put us up for the night."

"I don't think we can risk that," Seth said. "Whoever ambushed us could have picked us up in Bryson City, which means they may know exactly who your uncle is."

"Cherokee, then?" Rachel asked.

"If we circle around on Highway one-fifteen, we can be back in Bitterwood in four hours," Seth said.

"They'll know where to find us there, too," Rachel protested.

"I think my name is still good enough around Cooper Security to get us some help getting you out of town," Delilah said.

"What, you're going to ask your old company to fly the cavalry up here to the rescue?" Seth protested. "In this weather?"

"There's the cabin," Rachel said.

"If they know about your uncle, they probably know about the cabin," Seth disagreed. "But if we can get back to Bitterwood, we can take Rachel's car and drive out of town."

"Whatever we do, we may want to hurry," Brand murmured.

Delilah glanced his way. He was holding a cell phone, his expression grim in the reflected light from the display. "Are you crazy? The FBI can trace you to that phone!"

He looked up at her, his eyes glinting. "Not this phone. Trust me."

Right now she was feeling too paranoid to trust anyone. But she had more pressing problems at hand than whether or not the FBI would find him through his phone. "Why do we need to hurry?"

"The weather forecast says the snow's going to be worse than anticipated."

"How much worse?" Rachel asked, sounding worried.

"Well over a foot in the higher elevations," Brand said. "And as much as six inches even in the valleys."

Delilah's heart sank. Whatever way they took back to Bitterwood, they'd have to traverse some very high mountain passes. Her winter-driving skills were a little rusty these days, since she hadn't had to deal with much snow in Alabama over the past few years. "What are the snow parameters?"

"From west of Knoxville to Lenoir City, North Carolina."

In the backseat, Seth muttered a curse.

"How much time do we have before it gets really bad?" Rachel asked.

"The worst hits in an hour, but the situation is going to deteriorate steadily before then," Brand answered. "How far are we from anywhere that might offer lodgings?"

"Cherokee is twenty minutes from here in good conditions," Seth said. "Even adding time to account for the weather, we can be there in under an hour. I know a guy who runs a motel right on the highway. If he has any rooms available, he'll let us have them. He owes me."

Delilah squelched the urge to ask just what kind of debt Seth's friend owed him. Given her brother's colorful and often unsavory past, she didn't want to know. "Okay, Cherokee it is."

She checked the rearview mirror to make sure the mystery truck wasn't zooming up behind them. The highway in their taillights was dark and empty, while in their headlights, blowing snow was starting to pile up on the shoulder. It wouldn't be long until the cold white stuff started accumulating on the blacktop as well, Delilah knew.

She squelched the urge to put the pedal to the floorboard. As much as she wanted to get to Cherokee quickly, excessive speed in this weather was a damned good way to end up dead.

Still, they entered the Cherokee Indian Reservation within thirty minutes, and not long after that, Seth pointed out a single-story brown brick building that looked like apartments. A fading white sign at the front of the building read Come Stay Inn.

"This is it?" Delilah asked, her heart sinking.

"It's better on the inside," Seth assured her, although he didn't sound as certain as she might have hoped.

She went with Seth to the office at the end of the building. All of the rooms appeared to be dark, but faint light emanated from the office. Inside they found a tall, narrow-faced man in his late thirties, with long, thinning black hair and deep brown eyes, manning the front desk. Beside him the only light was the hissing glow of a gas-powered lantern.

"Seth. Long time, brother."

"Donnie. This is my sister, Delilah. Dee, this is Donnie Sims, an old friend. Donnie, we need a couple of rooms for the night."

"You're in luck, sort of. I have one room left. Of course, the power's out, so I can't promise it'll be warm, but at least it'll be shelter."

"One room?" Delilah looked at her brother.

"Two beds," Donnie added helpfully.

"We'll take it," Seth said, returning her look with a slight shrug. He turned back to Donnie. "We'll need some extra blankets. What'll it cost us?"

Chapter Seven

"I'm sorry," Brand said.

Delilah turned her head from the motel-room window and looked at him. Power was still out, and they'd have to extinguish the borrowed gas lantern soon as well. At least Seth had coaxed enough extra blankets out of the innkeeper to keep them relatively warm during the winter storm.

"What are you sorry for?" Delilah tugged the blanket draped over her shoulders more tightly around her.

"For getting you any deeper into this mess."

She glanced toward the bed on the far side of the room. Seth and Rachel were curled up together, warmed by their bulky clothes and two extra blankets. "I'd be in it anyway. Someone's after Seth and Rachel. I don't even know which one."

"I got Seth into this mess, too."

"Rachel got him into it." She turned back to look at Brand, her lips curving in a slight smile. "He was already keeping an eye on her before you ever asked him to do it."

"Really?" Brand looked over at the two on the bed and lowered his voice. "Seems an odd pairing."

"The heart wants what it wants." She looked back to the window. No cars had passed in over an hour, but she'd stand watch all night if necessary. "What I don't get is why Cortland would still be targeting Rachel," she added, peering out at the falling snow.

"Maybe it's Seth he's targeting."

"But why?"

"Because Seth was working for me on this case."

Delilah turned to look at him again. "How would Cortland know?"

"I think someone's on Cortland's payroll. Either someone at the FBI or someone at the Bitterwood P.D."

"Any idea who?"

"I was hoping you might have an idea."

Frowning, she turned her gaze back to the window. "I've been wondering for a while whether someone at the police department could be on the take. It was too damned convenient that Paul Bailey died in the jail, for one thing. Whether he did it to himself or someone else killed him."

"And didn't you tell me it took a ridiculous amount of time for someone to connect those murders, even though three of the women had worked at the same company?"

"Right. The police seemed determined not to call them serial murders."

"Even then, nobody brought in outside help."

"If Ivy and Sutton hadn't done such a thorough job of putting the pieces together, I'm not sure Rachel would even be alive now." She glanced back at the bed across the room. Rachel's eyes were closed and she seemed to be sleeping, but Seth's green eyes were open, watching them.

"I guess you have questions," she said to Seth, keeping her voice low so as not to awaken Rachel.

"A few," he answered just as quietly, his gaze slanting toward Brand. "But they can wait." He rested his chin atop Rachel's head, spooned her closer and shut his eyes.

Brand's hand closed over her wrist, drawing her attention back to him. He nodded toward the window.

Delilah looked out and saw a large black truck driving slowly toward the motel, its headlights slicing through the heavy snowfall. Her gut tightened to a knot as she and Brand each rolled away from the window, flattening their backs against the wall on either side.

The headlights briefly illuminated the room through the space in the curtains, then passed. Delilah peeked through the curtains, getting a good look at the back of the truck as it went by. It was the Ram 3500, with the same mud-covered license plate with half the numbers obscured.

Thank God, she thought, that Brand had suggested parking the Camaro behind the motel, out of sight of the road. If the people in that truck had seen the Camaro parked in front of the room, they might have decided to shoot up the motel first and ask questions later.

"Do you think they know we're here?"

"I think they know we're connected with Seth and Rachel," Brand answered. "Maybe they're assuming we went to Bryson City to shelter with Rachel's family there."

"That means her uncle and aunt may be in danger." She looked back at the bed and saw both Rachel and Seth staring back at her.

"I have to call him," Rachel said, wriggling out of Seth's grasp. "I have to warn him."

"They might have a trace on your phone," Brand warned.

Delilah looked at him, frowning. "Can Cortland do that?"

"He got someone to spoof my emails so well that the FBI still hasn't seen through the subterfuge."

"Who's Cortland?" Seth asked.

"I have to call my uncle now," Rachel said firmly, freeing herself from the bedcovers and rising to her feet.

"Here." Brand pulled his phone from his pocket and slid it across the bed to Rachel. She picked it up and started dialing.

"No details," Delilah warned. "Just tell him someone ambushed you and you think it's possible they'll come looking for you in Bryson City."

As Rachel started talking to her uncle, Seth wandered over to where Delilah and Brand stood, his eyes hooded with wariness. "What are we into here, Agent Brand?" There wasn't much in the way of respect in Seth's use of Brand's title, as far as Delilah could tell. Her brother was angry, though he'd long ago learned to control his rage by hiding it behind a mask of sarcasm.

"I'm sorry, Seth. I didn't know when this all started just how ugly it would get. I never would have brought you into this if I had."

"Yeah. Heard that one from you before." He glanced across the room at Rachel, who was still talking to her uncle while pacing in a tight, tense circle. "I can't take her back to Bitterwood, and clearly I can't take her to Bryson City, either. Any suggestions?"

Delilah looked at Brand. "I think we call Cooper Security in on this, like I suggested before. Jesse can provide a safe house and some guards for them."

"I'm guessing he'd be willing to give you a family-and-friends discount on this one." Brand glanced out the window again, his brow furrowed. "The last thing I saw from the weather report, the snow should end before daybreak and the worst should melt off by tomorrow afternoon. Cooper could chopper up here and take the three of you back to Alabama by tomorrow night."

Delilah stared at him, realizing what he was suggesting. "The *three* of us?"

Brand's blue eyes met hers. "I can't go. I'm a fugitive. It could cost Cooper his business and probably his freedom to help me out."

"So—what? You keep running and we go into hiding?"

"I have to prove my innocence."

"Do you have to do it alone?"

He glanced past her at Seth, then at Rachel on the phone. "I've put all of you in enough danger."

"How do you even know this has anything to do with what happened to you?" Seth asked. "Somebody's been gunning for Rachel for a while. Somebody her stepbrother owed money to. We hoped it was over, but—"

"That somebody, I believe, is a man named Wayne Cortland."

"Who?" Rachel crossed to the window and handed Brand his phone.

"Did you reach your uncle okay?"

She nodded. "He and Aunt Jeanine are going to bug out. He didn't tell me where. I didn't ask."

Delilah lifted an eyebrow. "Bug out?"

"He was a marine for fifteen years," Rachel said. "They have contingency plans for everything."

"Who is Wayne Cortland?" Seth asked.

"That," Brand said wearily, "is a long, sordid story."

DELILAH MANAGED TO get some sleep that night, though it was fitful and plagued with dreams. She woke to the first gray light of dawn trickling through the motel-room window and a warm body pressed firmly against her back. Blinking away sleep, she spotted her brother at the window, sprawled in a chair with his jeans-clad legs stretched out in front of him. As she stirred, he turned his head slowly to look at her. "Mornin'."

She sat up and looked at the bed beside her. Brand was stretched out, his back to her, his chest rising and falling in a slow, even cadence. She eased off the bed without waking him and dropped into the cheap chair opposite her brother. "When did he finally go to bed?"

"A couple of hours ago. I told him I'd keep watch." He

checked out the window again, moving the curtains just enough for Delilah to see that the winter storm had left a heavy covering of snow across the parking lot. "Are you sure you don't want to come to the safe house with us?"

"Brand can't do this by himself. Not with someone gunning for him. He needs someone to watch his back."

"Someone like you?" Seth's left eyebrow ticked upward.

"I've done it before."

He lowered his voice. "What happened between you two?"

"I'd had enough of the FBI, so I left." It was a grossly simplified version of what had really happened, but it was true enough.

"I get the feeling there's more."

"It doesn't matter what happened before. He's clearly being framed now. There's no way in hell Adam Brand would do the things he's been accused of. And he needs someone to help him prove it."

"And, again, that someone would be you?"

"I have the experience. I know this part of the world. And I believe him. I'm the best possible person to help him."

"What about your new job?"

She frowned at her brother. "Delivering justice is part of my job, isn't it? Wayne Cortland manipulated Paul Bailey into ordering the murders of four women and a man in order to get his hands on Davenport Trucking. Those four murders happened in Bitterwood, not Maryville, which makes them Bitterwood P.D. business."

"Think your new bosses at the police department will concur?"

"I have almost a week before I start there. I can give Brand at least that much, can't I?"

"I can't ask it."

Seth and Delilah both turned at the sound of Brand's deep

voice. He sat up in the bed, his hand pressed against his injured side.

"We should change your bandage," Delilah said, crossing to him.

Brand shrugged off his jacket and lifted the hem of the sweater beneath. The bandage was a little rumpled around the edges, but there didn't seem to be much bloody ooze seeping through it.

"How's it look?"

"Better, actually. Maybe we dodged that infection bullet after all." She changed the bandage quickly, having become skilled at the task over the past couple of days. With Seth as an audience, she managed to keep her head, but even her brother's presence wasn't quite enough to render her immune to Brand's physical attractions.

It had been a mistake to kiss him last night in the car, even though the circumstances had demanded it. Kissing him had brought back a flood of memories she'd spent the past eight years trying to exorcise.

They fit. Their bodies, their mouths, their minds. She'd never fit so well with anyone in her life, and if she was any good at reading people, she knew he felt the same way. But it hadn't kept him from cutting her off and, ultimately, sending her away.

He'd wanted her, without a doubt. But not enough to make the changes in his life that would make it possible for the two of them to be together.

"I don't want you to put your life on the line for me," he murmured as she taped down the last strip of adhesive.

"It's not your call."

"It *is* my call."

She leveled a look at him that made him blink. "You have no control over what I do or don't do. Not anymore."

His eyes narrowed. "So you're just going to throw yourself in front of the diesel engine barreling down the tracks at me?"

"I'm going to find the truth. Wherever it takes me."

He touched her face, a brief brush of fingertips along her jaw, then dropped his hand to his lap. "I'm not going to talk you out of this, am I?"

"No."

He took a deep breath and looked over at Seth, who was watching them with his eyebrows slightly elevated. "You and Rachel agree we call Cooper Security to get you out of here?"

Seth's gaze slid over to take in his sleeping girlfriend, then met Brand's gaze again. "Yes."

"I've been thinking about that," Delilah said, drawing Brand's attention back to her. "You said someone spoofed your emails so well that even the FBI is having trouble identifying them as fake, right?"

"Yes." Brand looked grim. "I told you Cortland's been making connections with anarchists. Some of them are hacktivists."

"Hacktivists?" Seth asked.

"Hackers with a political agenda. In this case, toward anarchistic ends."

"Those guys in the truck got my license number, surely," Delilah said. "They've probably already hacked into the Alabama DMV to find out who I am and where I worked."

"And they might already have a watch on Cooper Security," Brand said with a grimace, following her thoughts.

"There may be a way around it, though."

"Yeah?" Seth asked.

"There are a whole lot of Coopers in Alabama. One branch of the family runs a fishing campground and marina. I can get in touch with one of them, using your burner phone. They can relay the message to Jesse Cooper and arrange for an evac without going through official Cooper Security channels. I can even relay the message in Cooper Security code for an extra layer of security."

Brand held out his phone. "Do it."

"First, a question. Has anyone checked the latest on the weather? Any idea how soon we might get enough melt-off to drive out of here?"

Brand took the phone back and used it to check the weather. "Temperature's already hovering around the freezing mark. Should be in the forties by midmorning, and full sun. Could have a decent amount of melt-off by lunchtime. Enough to make for good driving. And once we get out of the snow zone, it should be clear all the way." He handed her the phone.

She thought for a moment, pondering which Cooper would be the least likely to draw scrutiny. Then she dialed a number she'd memorized years ago, when she'd had to relay a message to Jesse Cooper without going through channels on a surveillance job that had gone spectacularly wrong.

A woman's voice answered on the third ring. "Whoever you are, it's four a.m. and I'm seven months pregnant. This had better be spectacularly good."

"Abby, it's Delilah Hammond."

"Oh." There was a rustle on the other end of the line as Abby Cooper apparently sat up in bed. "Hi. Is something wrong? I thought you left town."

"I did. But I need a favor." As briefly as she could, she explained the situation without mentioning Brand. "I need Jesse to send an evacuation team as soon as possible to get my brother and his girlfriend out of harm's way and put them in a safe house until I can track down who's targeting them."

"Of course. But why didn't you call Jesse directly?"

"I have reason to suspect someone may be monitoring Cooper Security communications. Jesse needs to know that, too, and put Shannon on closing any possible loopholes."

"Okay. Listen, Luke wants to talk to you." Abby passed the phone to her husband.

Luke Cooper's voice was alert and serious. "Tell me what you need and we'll get it to you."

Spoken like a marine, Delilah thought with a smile. The long-lost Cooper brother had returned to the family fold a few years earlier after realizing his go-it-alone policy against the ruthless drug lord gunning for him was putting people he loved in danger. While his current career was running a riding stable that provided horses for tourists vacationing in the Cooper Cabins on Gossamer Ridge, he was one man the people of Chickasaw County could depend on in a righteous fight.

If anyone could make sure Seth and Rachel got to safety, it was Luke.

She gave him the code to deliver to Jesse, which included coordinates for a rendezvous point near Pilot Mountain, North Carolina, a town about four hours east of Cherokee. Luke and some of his brothers had made friends with a farmer who'd let them land the Cooper Security helicopter on his property during a manhunt a couple of years ago. He'd probably let them land there again.

"When can you be there?"

Delilah calculated the drive. Four hours to Pilot Mountain, and based on the latest weather information, they should be able to leave the motel by noon at the latest. "I think we can be there at seventeen hundred," she said, using military time by habit, since that was Jesse Cooper's habit as well. Five hours would allow for travel difficulties on the first leg of the trip and still give them time to make it to Pilot Mountain to meet the chopper.

"How many passengers?"

She looked at Brand. "Two."

"We'll be there." Luke hung up.

Delilah gave Brand the phone. "I think that phone's just about lost its usefulness for us."

"I have another burner. Clean as a whistle and untraceable to me."

She shook her head. "How long have you suspected you'd have to bug out like this?"

"Long enough." He looked at Seth. "We won't be able to keep in touch once you're out of here."

Seth met his sister's gaze. "I know."

"I wish we had time to let Mama know what's going on," Delilah said with regret.

"Bad time for everyone to abandon her." Seth frowned. "Do you think this Cortland person will go after her to get to us?"

Delilah's gut turned a flip. She hadn't even considered that possibility. "We need to get her to safety, too. If we can get to Sutton, he could do it. He still has contacts at Cooper Security."

"I know who could give him a message," Seth said.

"Who?"

"Cleve."

Delilah met her brother's gaze with apprehension. "Can he communicate now?"

"Well enough. All I have to do is tell him my mother may be in danger and Sutton needs to take care of her. Cleve will tell him. And Sutton will do it. He'll do it for you, if not for me."

"What then?" Delilah asked. "He's going to stash her with him and Ivy at Ivy's place for God knows how long?"

"Only a few days," Brand said quietly, making both Delilah and Seth look at him.

"A few days?" Delilah felt a shiver of anger at his cool calm. This was her mother they were talking about, and maybe Reesa Hammond hadn't been a candidate for parent of the year, but she deserved protection. "How can you know it'll only be a few days?"

"Because as soon as we drop off Seth and Rachel, we're heading to Virginia."

"To Cortland's neck of the woods?" Seth asked, puzzled.

"Exactly," Brand answered with a jut of his jaw. "I can't run the rest of my life. If we're going to prove my innocence, it won't be by running away."

"What are you saying?" Delilah asked, half scared, half excited to hear his answer.

Brand's gaze locked with hers, his blue eyes hard with determination. "I'm saying, we take the fight to him. One way or another, we're going to end this thing."

Chapter Eight

"I hope Cleve got the message to Sutton about my mother."

Brand opened his eyes, jarred from a light doze by Delilah's first words in several miles. "Seth seems to think Cleve can be trusted."

"Cleve is a con man."

"Used to be. Now he's an old man trying to recover from a stroke." He shifted in the passenger seat, wincing as the healing wound in his side pulled with the movement. "And whatever his reasons, he has a soft spot for Seth."

She glanced his way, eyes narrowed. "How do you know so much about Cleve and Seth? I never talked about Cleve Calhoun back in the day."

"I've been in touch with Seth since then, remember."

She looked back at the highway unfolding in front of them. They were heading north on I-74, toward the Virginia state line. They'd waited with Seth and Rachel until the Bell LongRanger helicopter had shown up with a small army of Coopers to escort Delilah's brother and his girlfriend to a Cooper Security safe house. Brand had stayed in the Camaro, crouched out of sight, until the chopper had lifted off, heading southwest into the waning sunlight.

"Why did you contact Seth, really?" Delilah asked quietly a few minutes later. "Were you spying on me through him?"

Brand felt a flutter of guilt, because that had been exactly why he'd made contact with Seth five years ago. He'd been able to keep track of Delilah, at a distance, when she'd worked as an investigator for the Commonwealth's Attorney in Norfolk, Virginia. But Delilah had left that job after three years to work for Cooper Security, and Brand's connection to Jesse Cooper's outfit had been limited to Cooper's sister, Isabel, who'd been on his team at the FBI.

Isabel was the soul of discretion, not prone to gossip or sharing her brother's business—or that of his employees— with anyone else, save perhaps with Ben Scanlon, her partner and now her husband.

So he'd been forced to make contact with Seth instead.

He'd planned, quite ruthlessly, to make a few threats in order to get the con man's cooperation in keeping an eye on Delilah. But as it turned out, Seth Hammond had been ready to make a change in his life, and instead of strong-arming Seth into cooperating, he'd ended up helping the man get out of the con game and into honest, if sometimes dangerous, work.

"Not going to answer?" Delilah prodded.

"I was spying on you through him," Brand admitted.

He couldn't tell by her expression whether she found his answer satisfying or annoying. Maybe a little of both, he realized as the conflicting emotions played out a skirmish in her dark eyes.

"I wanted to make sure you were okay," he added.

Annoyance won the battle. "Feeling guilty, were you?"

He felt a touch of annoyance himself. "I'm not the one who told you to leave the FBI."

"You made it impossible for me to stay."

"What did you want from me?"

"I just wanted—" She stopped short, a pained expression on her face as she flattened her lips into a thin line. "I guess

I wanted something impossible. And I couldn't go back to the way it was before."

He didn't have to ask, *Before what?* He knew the night everything had changed as well as she did. He'd just been hoping they could compartmentalize that night, hide it away like a keepsake, remembered only in passing but not part of their daily existence.

She'd been the one who had said, in unequivocal terms, that she couldn't pretend what had happened between them hadn't happened. She couldn't shove those feelings inside her every day and go about the job as if they were nothing more than colleagues.

He'd thought he could, but in hindsight, he wondered if he would have been successful.

He wanted her, even now. More than he had anticipated.

He changed the topic, looking for more common ground. "Have you thought any more about our plan?"

"What plan? Best I can tell, our plan is to drive up to Travisville, holler 'Yoo-hoo, we're over here' and start ducking when the bullets start flying."

"Technically, we don't duck until we figure out where the bullets are coming from."

She rolled her eyes so hard, they nearly turned a 360-degree flip.

"It's significant, I think, that he's still going after Rachel Davenport."

"He might be going after Seth instead," she pointed out.

"It doesn't make much sense that he's going after either of them," Brand conceded. "Unless Cortland has made the connection between Seth and me."

"So he's what? Trying to isolate you? Make sure you don't have anywhere you can go to ground?"

"It's not a secret at the FBI that I've been using your brother as a confidential informant."

"Which would mean someone at the bureau is on Cortland's payroll."

"Wouldn't have to be anyone high up the chain," Brand pointed out. "Like I said, my work relationship with Seth isn't classified information there. Anyone in payroll or even the clerical workers in the office would know about Seth."

"It won't be hard for Cortland's men in the truck to run my license plate and connect me to you, either. Since we worked together at the FBI for a few years." Delilah grimaced. "Maybe we should both do something about changing our appearances."

He slanted his head to one side, considering her appearance. Since her days in the FBI, she'd let her hair grow long and stopped adding honey-gold highlights, allowing her hair to go back to its natural dusky color. "When was the last time you had a photograph taken?"

She shrugged, frowning. "I have an internal photo with my file at Cooper Security, but that's considered eyes only, since I did a lot of undercover work. Jesse assured me when I resigned that my files will remain sealed. I guess the last time I had a photo taken was when I was working at the Commonwealth Attorney's office in Norfolk." She grimaced. "God, I hope they got rid of that photo."

"Why?"

"Well, I was trying to put the FBI behind me, that whole corporate bureaucracy thing, and I was doing some undercover investigations, so I chopped my hair off short and dyed it bright red. That's the picture that was on my official department ID."

When this mess was over, he thought with a hidden smile, he was going to have to hunt down someone in the Commonwealth Attorney's office and get his hands on that photo. "What about your driver's-license photo?"

"Oh, God, nobody would recognize me from that monstrosity." She made a face. "I had to rush to get the license renewed in the middle of an undercover assignment about three years ago. I was dolled up like a two-buck prostitute on an eight-day crack binge."

"So, basically, if someone went looking for a photo of you from the last eight years, it would look nothing like you look now?"

"Pretty much. The photo at Cooper would come the closest, but I don't see Jesse giving out that kind of information to anyone."

Brand didn't like the idea floating through his head at the moment, even though it made a great deal of sense. If Cortland didn't know what she looked like, she might be able to go within spitting distance of his lair and never be noticed. With her familiarity with the hills, her local accent and her chameleonlike ability to blend into the background, she was the perfect person to send into Travisville to do a little reconnaissance.

"You have an idea but you don't want to tell me about it." She gave him an exasperated look that transported him back eight years.

"Cortland doesn't leave Travisville if he can help it." Brand looked at the road ahead of them. Outside metropolitan areas, the traffic on the interstate highways was light enough for easy navigation, but he still felt naked, as if every vehicle they passed might contain an occupant who knew what he looked like and what he was wanted for. "The people he hires come to him. So if we want to figure out what he's up to—"

"We have to go to Cortland," she finished for him.

"I'm not putting your neck on the line for me." He shook his head. "I won't ask you to do this, Hammond. It scares me sick to think about it."

"I know it does." She reached out and touched his arm, her fingers strong and warm. "But I'm already neck deep in this mess. Cortland went after my brother. He'll be after me as well, even if I do nothing."

"You don't know that."

"Really?" Her dark eyes gleamed with skepticism. "Look at the lengths this guy has gone to already. We're in the way of whatever he has planned. All of us. There's no way in hell I can stay on the sidelines."

She was right. He knew it. He just didn't want to believe there wasn't a way to keep her safe.

She squeezed his arm, then let go. "We need to know what he's up to, not just to stop him from coming after us, but to stop him from doing whatever he has planned."

His skin still tingled where she'd touched him. "Any ideas how we go about that?"

"A few," she admitted. Then she flashed him a sassy grin so familiar it made his breath catch. "But first, Special Agent Brand, you need to feed me. Because I'm starving."

"WHY DID HE pick Oak Ridge National Laboratory, I wonder?" Delilah asked an hour later over burgers and sodas they'd bought at a fast-food place in Mount Airy. They'd pulled the Camaro into a slot in a strip-mall parking lot while they ate.

"It would certainly raise a lot of warning flags for the feds," Brand pointed out, stretching his legs gingerly. The Camaro wasn't built for men his size, Delilah thought with sympathy. "They take nuclear security pretty damned seriously, for obvious reasons."

"Which makes it an odd choice for a federal agent gone rogue, doesn't it?" she asked. "You of all people would know how hard it would be to accomplish what you're accused of plotting."

"True. And the Surry and North Anna plants in Virginia are closer to my home base."

"So maybe there's a reason why Cortland chose Oak Ridge."

Brand slanted a look at her. "You mean he has plans for the place himself?"

"He's hanging out with militias and anarchists, either of which group might want to create the kind of havoc an attack on a nuclear laboratory could produce."

"But what's in it for Cortland? I don't get the idea that this guy's a true believer, even if he's got his minions convinced otherwise. There has to be a profit angle in it for him to go to these lengths."

"Okay, so who profits from an attack on Oak Ridge?"

"Well, any time something happens at a nuclear plant, the whole industry comes under scrutiny."

"So if the nuclear industry comes under scrutiny, the winners in that scenario are other energy producers, right?"

"Right. Coal, hydroelectric, oil, natural gas."

"Does Cortland have any energy holdings?"

Brand shook his head. "No. He has land connected to his lumberyard, and probably some logging interests, but no energy holdings that I know of."

"Maybe they're under another name," Delilah suggested, stifling a yawn. "Before we leave Mount Airy, maybe I should go to the local library and do a little research."

"I have a better idea," Brand said.

She looked up to find his gaze directed toward the large navy-and-white Walmart sign glowing in the deepening twilight. "Yeah?"

"Why borrow a computer for an hour or two when you can own one?"

"You have that kind of cash to toss around?"

"We can get a tablet for under five hundred."

"We can eat about fifty times for that kind of money."

He grinned. "I forgot what a thrifty little thing you always were."

"Seriously, we can borrow the library computer for free, probably. I'll just have to show my ID to get a guest pass or something."

"And every time you flash your ID, it's one more chance for Cortland to track you down." Brand dug in the pocket of his jeans and pulled out a fat money clip. "Meanwhile, take this with you into the store, buy a tablet with cash, and nobody's going to ask to see your ID at all." He peeled off five hundred-dollar bills and handed them to her. "Go ahead. I'll wait here for you."

She looked at the money clip, wondering just how many more hundreds he had folded up in it.

"I saw this mess coming for a while," he said quietly, drawing her gaze up to meet his. His blue eyes were hard with regrets. "I wasn't sure how it would shake out, but I figured I'd best prepare for the worst."

"I'm sorry all of this happened to you. I know how much you prided yourself in the job." The memory of just how seriously he took his job, and the price he was willing to pay to keep it, still had the power to make her heart ache.

"I'm going to get to the bottom of this mess." There wasn't a hint of doubt in his voice.

Delilah stifled a smile. His confidence had always been his most alluring asset as far as she was concerned. She'd sensed immediately that he was a man who appreciated confidence in the people he worked with, so she'd tamped down her fears and thrown a whole boatload of confidence right back in his face when she'd walked into his office and informed him that she planned to be the next member of his domestic-terrorism task force.

She wondered if he'd had any idea just how hard her knees had been shaking that day.

"I'll be back as soon as I can." She reached over and plucked the dark blue baseball cap from his head. "Mind if I borrow this?"

She didn't wait for an answer, pulling the cap over her head and tucking her hair up under the band. She tugged the bill low over her face, zipped her hoodie up to her neck and hurried across the parking lot to the front of the discount department store.

"Too bad you couldn't wait a couple of weeks," the cashier at the front commented as she scanned the tablet computer Delilah had selected. "Black Friday, we're probably going to drop this price by twenty-five percent."

"It's for a birthday," Delilah lied. "Can't wait until Thanksgiving." She'd also picked up some clothes for herself and a small duffel bag in which to stash them, since the tablet didn't take up the whole five hundred dollars and she'd been wearing the same clothes for entirely too long. She handed over the cash, noting the woman's slightly arched eyebrows as she spotted the hundred-dollar bills.

She took them without comment, however, and handed Delilah the change and a receipt. "Have a nice night."

"You, too," Delilah returned politely, already halfway to the exit.

The parking lot was nearly full, and there were enough shoppers milling about to give Delilah a prickly sensation at the back of her neck. But a casual look around the parking lot assured her nobody was paying much attention to her at all.

Back at the Camaro, she stopped one more time outside the driver's door and scanned the parking lot, looking for anything out of place. After a few seconds, she decided she was being paranoid and opened the car door.

She pulled the boxed tablet from her shopping bag and handed it to Brand as she slid behind the wheel. "I bought some clothes, too. Hope that's okay."

He slanted a look at her and grinned. "That's fine. You were starting to get a little ripe."

She made a face at him. "Now what?"

"Now we find us a free Wi-Fi hotspot and get this baby up and running."

"ANOTHER NIGHT, ANOTHER cheap motel." Freshly showered and dressed in sweatpants and a long-sleeved T-shirt she'd bought at Walmart, Delilah flopped on the only bed in the room, a queen-size job that had seen better days, but none of them recently. The motel was a boxy, halfhearted attempt at traveler lodging called Sleep and Save Inn, located a few miles west of Galax, Virginia. Its primary assets were a sleepy-looking desk clerk who didn't look twice at Brand's fake ID and, as advertised in neon letters on the motel marquee, free Wi-Fi available to lodgers.

Brand locked the door behind them and engaged the safety latch before he settled in one of the uncomfortable tub chairs by the window table. "Sorry there wasn't a room with two beds available. But I couldn't pass up free Wi-Fi. As long as we use other people's IP addresses, we'll be damned hard to track through the internet."

"Maybe we could table that until morning," she suggested, attempting to hold back an enormous yawn. "If we're heading to Travisville tomorrow, we should probably be well rested and alert."

"Good idea." He smiled as she stifled another yawn. "It's late, and I'm bushed. Why don't we catch a little shut-eye and start fresh in the morning?"

"Okay." She swung her feet off the bed and started to get up.

"Where are you going?" Brand asked.

She looked back at him. "I'll take the chair. You're too big to sleep in a chair all night."

"We can share the bed, Hammond. We did last night."

She couldn't stop one eyebrow from lifting. "Dressed for the arctic and sharing a room with my brother and his girl-friend."

"It's not like you're in a little lace nightie tonight," he pointed out pragmatically, waving his hand at her clothing.

"I like to think my feminine allure doesn't depend on lingerie."

"It doesn't," he replied with a wicked grin. "But I think we're both a little too tired to give in to temptation." He patted the bed, and after a brief pause, she sat down beside him.

He looked down at his attire. "I can live with the jeans, but do I have your permission to lose the sweater?"

"Give it to me. I'm cold."

He shrugged off his sweater, revealing a T-shirt beneath. Delilah wasn't sure whether she was relieved or disappointed. He handed her his discarded sweater and she slipped it over her head, trying not to breathe in his scent too obviously, even though the familiar smell of him threatened to over-whelm her.

God, she'd missed him. Missed the sight of him, the smell of him, the sound of his voice and the timbre of his laugh. She'd thought—she'd hoped—that eight years away from him would have been enough to exorcise the memories, but they seemed to be imprinted on her at the cellular level, impossible to shake.

She wished they weren't bone tired and in the middle of a dangerous mess, that they didn't have a painful history or bleak hopes for any sort of future. She wished she could forget about yesterday and tomorrow and think only about tonight, about the feel of his body over her, under her, inside her.

But she couldn't forget, nor did he seem inclined to do so.

And the last thing she needed was another shattering memory of Adam Brand indelibly etched on her soul.

He lay back on the pillows and shut off the bedside lamp, plunging the motel room into dark. After a few seconds, Delilah's eyes adjusted to the low light enough to see the faint yellow glow of the sodium-vapor parking-lot lamps seeping through the heavily lined curtains of the room.

The night was a heavy kind of quiet, broken only by the sporadic traffic sounds coming from the highway nearby, the hum of electricity running through the walls and the staccato duet of their own breathing.

Unable to stand the silence any longer, she asked, "Do you ever see any of the old gang?"

"No," he answered. "I was the last one of the old crew left. Most of the others moved on to lead their own teams."

She might have done so as well, she thought, had she stuck around.

"How much do you know about the things I asked your brother to do for me?" he asked a few tense moments later.

"Not much. He keeps a lot to himself."

"I pushed him, maybe farther than I should have." Brand sounded regretful. "But I wanted him to see that he had it in him to be a hero."

Delilah smiled at the darkness. "A hero, huh? Don't you know that's a quaint, antiquated notion in this cynical world?"

"This cynical world has its share of heroes. But it could use more. I could tell Seth wanted to make up for his mistakes. And he was your brother, so I knew he had it in his genes to be one of the good guys."

"You never knew our father." She'd kept most of her past where it belonged—miles and years behind her. She and Brand had been close in a lot of ways, but there were parts of her experiences she'd never shared with him, just as she knew there were parts of his past that he'd kept from her, too.

Brand was silent for a long moment before he spoke. "I know a lot more about him than I ever told you."

She couldn't say she was surprised. As her supervisor, he'd have made it his business to know everything in her employment file, including the details of her background check. "Then you know he hit my mama, all the time. And she took it without sayin' much, because if he was hittin' her, he wasn't hittin' us." She grimaced as she heard her accent broaden, as if even thinking about her past transported her back to the days when she was little Dee Hammond from Smoky Ridge, whose daddy was a drug dealer and whose mama was a drunk. "She drank to dull the pain and kill the fear. Then, after he died, she drank to drown the guilt."

"Guilt? For what happened to your father?"

"For what happened to Seth."

"Seth was burned in the explosion and fire?"

"Mom had passed out drunk in the back bedroom, and somehow the explosion didn't tear that room apart like the rest of the house. Seth went back in there to get her. They both got out, but Seth had some painful burns on his back and chest. He probably still has the scars."

"Where were you?"

"At school. I stayed late every chance I got, because it was so much better than being at home."

Brand didn't say anything else for a long time. Delilah was relieved, frankly. She never felt any sort of catharsis from talking about her past, only a bitter film of regret that she'd ever lived it.

The silence extended so long she had started to doze off. When Brand spoke, it jarred her awake.

"I told you I was married before."

"Yes," she said, stifling a yawn.

"To another agent."

"Right." The FBI, unlike a lot of law-enforcement agencies, didn't have any rules about agents dating and marrying, beyond the obvious strictures against superiors having sexual relationships with agents under their supervision. Brand and his first wife, Joanna Lake, had been at the same level on the bureau totem pole, from what she'd learned through the FBI grapevine. They'd wed quickly and divorced quickly, the marriage not lasting a full year.

"Joanna seemed absolutely perfect for me. She was attractive, smart, funny, and being a fellow agent, she understood the pressures of the job. We had fun together. We were strongly attracted to each other. It seemed the perfect relationship for a couple of FBI agents still young enough and starry-eyed enough to believe in forever."

She asked the question she'd never asked before. "So what happened?"

She heard his intake of breath, as if preparing to answer. But before he could say a word, another sound pierced the quiet of the motel room.

A rattle of metal on metal.

Delilah whipped her head to the left, her gaze settling on the faint glow outside the lined window curtains. A shadow darkened one patch of the light, swaying slightly.

Someone was trying to open the motel-room door.

Chapter Nine

Brand grabbed the Ruger, still in its holster, from the bedside table, while Delilah went for her own weapon on the table near the window.

"Be careful!" he whispered as she moved toward the door and took a quick look through the peephole.

After a few seconds, she whispered, "I think it's a drunk. Probably has the wrong room." Raising her voice, she asked, "Who's there?"

The rattling of the doorknob ceased and a slurred male voice responded, muffled by the door. "Who are you?"

"I asked first," Delilah called.

There was a brief pause, then the slurred voice asked, "Is this room two sixteen?"

"No, it's one sixteen."

There was a babble of curses on the other side of the door. "Sorry! So sorry!" The shadow moved away from the door, weaving its way past the window.

Delilah slumped against the door, breathing hard. "This fugitive thing is for the birds."

"Tell me about it."

"We can't stay here any longer." She pushed away from the door and started picking up their things.

Brand set the Ruger back on the bedside table. "It was just a drunk—"

"What if it wasn't? Or even if it was, what if the next rattle on the door comes with a few bullet holes? You know how this works, Brand. Fugitives who stay free the longest are the ones who keep moving."

"We'll go in the morning." He caught her by the wrist as she came around the bed in search of something.

She went still, looking down at his hand. When she looked back at him, her eyes glittered in the low light. "How did they do this to you? Why did the FBI buy the allegations against you? You're a veteran FBI agent with a jacket full of commendations—"

"The shake-up in the administration after the president's chief of staff was implicated in a murder conspiracy was like an earthquake in the capital. We all felt the aftershocks." He thought about letting go of her wrist, but she didn't show any signs of wanting to get away. So he held on. "Even a whiff of potential corruption is taken very seriously these days. No exceptions."

"But how hard could it be for the FBI to ascertain that those emails were faked?"

"Very hard, if it's done well." He edged over and let go of her hand, patting the bed beside him.

She sat down, her hip warm against his. "The hacktivists you were talking about, right?"

He nodded. "The government's been known to hire some of them just to get them to stop making things hard for the good guys."

"Surely the FBI is putting some of their best guys on the task of proving you innocent."

"I don't think I helped spur them along by disappearing."

Her hand covered his in the dark. "Are you sure you're making the right decision, running this way?"

"If you were the one with your whole life on the line, what would you do? Stay in custody somewhere and depend on other people to save your life?" He turned his hand palm up, grasping her hand in his. "Tell the truth."

She was silent for a long moment. Then she squeezed his hand. "I wouldn't do that. I'd want to be the one looking for the truth."

He tugged her hand to his mouth, brushing his lips across her knuckles. "That's the decision I made, too."

"I still think we need to get out of here."

"Let's get some sleep while we can. It may be a while before we get the chance again." He scooted over on the bed, tugging her toward him. She resisted for a moment, then gave in, lying beside him.

She rolled onto her side, facing him in the dark. "You never finished telling me what happened between you and Joanna. How did it fall apart?"

He resisted the temptation to roll over and refuse to answer, even though a part of him, the private, self-protective part, begged him to do so. She'd shared a painful, private story about her own life. The least he owed her was a little honesty about his own checkered past.

"We married too fast. We mistook surface compatibility and sexual attraction for something with a chance to last. But despite all the things we had in common, we didn't want the same things in life."

"Like what?"

"Joanna wanted a big house on the Chesapeake Bay. A golden retriever and two kids playing in the big backyard and a nanny to watch them while we worked. She wanted me to take every promotion opportunity that came my way, even if it was a position that held no interest for me. For her, the job was about the income and the advancement opportunities. Not the hunt."

"You didn't know that before you married?"

"Maybe I knew it but just didn't want to admit it. Maybe

I thought once we were building a life together, we'd both bend a little toward the middle. But it turned out neither of us was willing to bend at all."

"So you broke."

"Yeah. I guess we were luckier than most. No kids to screw up, no house to divide. We signed the papers, wished each other good luck and went our separate ways."

"No harm, no foul?" She sounded skeptical.

"It hurt. My ego more than my heart, perhaps. But I learned a hard lesson about mixing business and pleasure."

"Lots of FBI agents have very good marriages with fellow agents." She spoke cautiously, as if she had her doubts about the feasibility of intra-agency fraternization herself.

"They do. I'm just not sure it was something I was capable of."

She fell quiet long enough for him to wonder if she'd drifted off to sleep. But in a few moments, her sleepy voice broke the silence. "Was that why you cut things off between us after West Virginia?"

It had certainly been part of it. "I didn't want things between us to change. If we'd tried to build on what happened that night, things would have changed drastically. The whole team dynamic would have shifted."

"And you were my superior agent."

"Yes. To make it work, you'd have had to be reassigned."

"So instead, you just told me what happened could never happen again." Her voice was carefully neutral, but he knew her well enough to recognize a darker thread of pain beneath the measured tone.

"And you left."

"You valued the team dynamic more than you valued what happened between the two of us."

Valued wasn't exactly the right word, but he wasn't sure

she'd see the distinction. "What we were doing on the domestic-terrorism task force at the time was vital to national security."

"But you lost me from the team anyway."

He vividly remembered walking into his office to find her sitting there, a transfer request in her hand, her back as stiff as steel and her eyes blazing pain and rage in equal parts. "Yes."

"If you'd said something, anything, that day I told you about the transfer—"

A part of him had regretted his silence for a lot of years. But regrets were cheap. They didn't have the power to change much of anything. And he'd been certain he was doing the right thing.

Was he still certain? Being here with her, seeing her again, feeling the heat of her body next to his and hearing her familiar voice, he found his previous certainty crumbling.

He'd missed her horribly, all these years. Hadn't really let her go, going so far as to use her brother to keep track of her. Were those the actions of a man who'd made the right decision?

Delilah rolled onto her back, the faint light seeping through the curtains casting her face in shades of gold. "I guess I thought you'd stop me."

I wanted to, he thought. But he didn't say it aloud. Then or now.

She shifted again, turning her back to him. He clenched his fists to keep from touching her.

I wanted to ask you to stay, he thought, staring at the curve of her shoulder, listening to the sound of her slow, steady breathing, an ache burning in the center of his chest. *More than I ever realized.*

But he hadn't. Then—or now.

THE SNOW HADN'T reached as far east as Galax but the cold was bitter to the bone, sending a shiver through Delilah early the next morning when she crossed the street from the motel to a small mom-and-pop breakfast place for coffee and fresh-baked cheese croissants.

She'd left Brand asleep, careful not to wake him when he looked so relaxed and free of care. He'd never looked his age, and even now, knocking on the door of his mid-forties, he looked a decade younger. Only a smattering of gray flecked the hair at his temples, and there was a hint of silver in the beard he hadn't been bothering to shave since he'd gone on the run, but the lines on his face gave him character, not age, and his fit, toned body would put most younger men to shame.

Sharing a bed with him after all this time, and trying to pretend it was nothing more than a necessary convenience, had led to a series of strange dreams. Erotic in some ways, terrifying in others, and all conspiring to keep her from getting much benefit from the hours of sleep she'd managed.

Brand was no longer in bed when she unlocked the motel-room door and entered. He was flattened against the wall, his Ruger in hand. He slumped when he recognized her. "Don't do that again."

She slapped the bag of croissants against his chest. "Sorry. You looked so peaceful asleep, I didn't want to wake you."

While she carried the two cups of coffee to the small table in front of the window, Brand opened the bag of croissants. "Where'd you find these?"

"Little shop across the street." She nodded toward the window as she sat and pulled the cover off one of the cups of coffee. "By the way, it's cold as hell outside."

He sat across from her. "The frost on the window was my first clue."

"I think we should stay here until checkout time at noon and get as much computer work done as we can. Agreed?"

He narrowed his eyes. "Not looking forward to heading into Travisville?"

"Well, no, but I'm not stalling. If we're going to figure this mess out, we need as much information about Cortland as we can get our hands on."

"I have my preliminary files on Cortland on a flash drive." He dug in the pocket of his jeans and pulled out his wallet. Inside, tucked in the loose-change pouch, he'd hidden a small, oval-shaped flash drive. "It's not a lot—Liz and I were still in the early stages of trying to figure out what Cortland was up to when he sent his goons to kill her and frame me."

"He must have spies everywhere."

"That's my theory."

After they finished off the coffee and croissants, Brand set up the tablet computer and handed over the flash drive. "Take a look at the files on the flash drive first, get up to speed. Let me know if you have questions." He stretched out on the bed and folded his hands behind his head, his gaze settling on her as she got to work.

Trying not to feel self-conscious, she plugged the flash drive into the tablet's USB port and scanned the files, making notes as she went. Brand's style of research tended toward the methodical, while she favored a more freewheeling, stream-of-consciousness way of pulling the disparate threads of research into a narrative that made sense to her. There were pluses and minuses to the way she did things, just as there were to Brand's preferred style of forming a theory.

They'd always done their best work together, blending their styles for a comprehensive picture of whatever mystery lay unsolved in front of them.

"What made Liz suspect Cortland in the first place?" she asked aloud.

"She originally started investigating militias in south-western Virginia, and his name came up in the periphery of her investigation. She probably wouldn't have thought twice about it, however, if she hadn't connected the militias to the meth mechanics in the area. When she realized they were running joint operations, and one of the area's top meth cookers just so happened to do business with Cortland, it caught her attention."

"How do the anarchists fit in?" She opened the file on the hacktivists Brand had mentioned, running down a list of known screen names to see if any looked familiar.

"There was a pipe-bomb attack on a post office in Roanoke. Nobody killed, but the ATF identified the pipe bomber through his bomb signature. It was a guy named Harold Petry, a member of the Blue Ridge Infantry. Problem was, nobody could figure out what the BRI had against the post office."

"Maybe any federal building would have done."

"There's a courthouse right there in Roanoke. Much bigger target." Brand shook his head. "Liz and I interviewed the victims and that's when we learned that one of the people injured by the bomb had most likely been the primary target, based on the placement of the bomb. And he told us right away the only person he knew who had anything against him was a guy he knew only from online, a gamer he'd come across who made a big deal of being a hacktivist. Went by the name 'systemg33k.' With threes instead of *e*'s in *geek*."

She slanted a look at him.

"I don't name 'em," he said with a grin. "Anyway, we followed up and found the real name of the hacktivist was Neil Posey, and he's a freelance information tech in the Abingdon area. Guess who happens to be one of his IT clients?"

She looked away from the list again. "Wayne Cortland?"

"Well, technically, Cortland Lumber. But yes."

She looked back at the list of names, searching until she found systemg33k. "So that's three strikes for Cortland."

"It can't be a coincidence."

"No, I agree. It can't." Her gaze settled on another name in the list of hackers Brand and Liz had compiled. Her eyes narrowed. "Where did you get these names?"

"It's a list our cybersecurity section came up with," Brand answered, pushing up to a sitting position. "Why? Have you found something?"

On the list, a few names below systemg33k, was the name "pwnst4r." Something about the screen name niggled Delilah's memory but she couldn't quite make it click. "No," she said finally. "One of the names tripped a switch in my brain, but it's not really going anywhere. Let's move on."

"Are you sure?"

"Yeah." She opened a different file, one named "BRI." Inside, she found a list of names and, next to the names, a dossier. Most were brief, but a few had more details. She scanned the list to see if she recognized any of the names, but none rang a bell. "BRI—Blue Ridge Infantry. They weren't around back when I was at the bureau."

"They're a new outfit, although some of the founders had roots in other militia groups. Apparently there was a schism in the old group between the older guys, who were practically Luddites, eschewing modern technology, and the newer guys, who wanted to use technology to advance their principles. The BRI is one of the new breed. We think that's how they hooked up with the anarchists."

"Both of them hate all forms of government, though for different reasons," she said with a nod. "Is BRI a white-power group?"

"Not as much as the groups they broke off from. I mean, I doubt they have any ethnic members, but their goals don't seem as focused on white-supremacy issues. They're more interested in undermining the U.S. government wherever possible."

Delilah shook her head. "Part of me sympathizes, a little

bit, with what drives these groups. I'm from the mountains, you know. We're not many of us big fans of government intrusion. It was an issue I had to deal with all the time working for the FBI. How much of what we were doing was too much, you know?"

Brand nodded. "After 9/11, we probably went too far in trying to empower the government to keep us safe. But so much of what we accomplished did stop terrorist attacks from taking place."

"At a hell of a cost to civil liberties."

"Granted."

She looked back at the list. "But these guys aren't trying to preserve civil liberties. They're trying to destroy the fabric of civil society. That's definitely not the answer."

"No, it's not." Brand swung his legs over the side of the bed and stood, bending over her shoulder to read the tablet screen.

He smelled good, she thought, allowing herself to take a deep breath. Warm and masculine, the scent as familiar as the memory of him that had haunted her for years.

"We never could figure out what they were up to." His deep voice rumbled in her ear. "It's like we have all the pieces in place, but we're missing the one big section of the puzzle that will help it all make sense."

"I have a feeling we're going to have to go to Travisville for the answer." She turned to look at him. His face was close, the beard he'd been allowing to grow now thick enough to hide most of his jawline. Her fingers itched to run through the crisp, dark hair, to pull him down for a kiss and feel that beard against her skin.

She was no more immune to him now, after all these years, than she had been when they'd worked together daily. Maybe less immune, since it had been a long time since she'd had to shore up her defenses against the daily onslaught of his virile magnetism.

His blue eyes met hers and darkened, and she knew he'd read her naked desire for him on her face. For a moment he hesitated, and she imagined she could hear his heart pounding in frantic tandem with her own.

Then he backed away and sat down, snapping the cord of tension between them. She turned back to the table, bristling with frustration.

She spent the next couple of hours going through the rest of the files on the flash drive, trying to draw together the disparate threads of the conspiracy behind Elizabeth Vaughn's death and the frame-up that had sent Brand on the run.

"I'd like to get my hands on a list of Wayne Cortland's holdings," she said finally, pushing up from the table to stretch her legs. "There doesn't seem to be anything here listing what he owns outside the lumber mill."

Brand, who'd settled back on the bed and now lay staring at the ceiling, turned his head toward her. "That's because we haven't found any holdings. We're pretty sure anything else he owns is hidden behind shell corporations."

She sighed. "We need a forensic accountant. And, it so happens, I know one of those."

"At Cooper Security?"

Delilah nodded. "Evie Cooper, Jesse's wife. She's an accountant, and since she's been working for Cooper Security, she's been brushing up on her forensic skills. She's gotten damned good at digging up bones."

"I suppose one more call to Luke Cooper won't kill us." With a sigh, Brand sat up and dug his burner phone from his pocket. "But we're going to have to lose this phone and pick up another before we leave town."

She took the phone from him. "How's your slush fund holding out?"

"We're good for now. And if it comes to it, I have more stashed in a safe place near Abingdon."

She dialed the number for Cooper Stables, rather than Luke's home address, figuring he'd be working by now. Luke answered on the third ring. "Cooper Stables."

"Luke, it's Delilah."

"Hey. How're you doing?"

"I'm fine. Everything okay with Seth and Rachel?"

"They're all set up. And hey, your mama's fine, too. Sutton and his girl have taken her in and they're keeping a close watch on her."

Relief rippled through her. "Thanks. That's a huge help."

"I assume you're not just calling for an update, though."

"No, I need to get in contact with Evie. I need her help with something." She glanced at the tablet screen, which currently displayed the contents of the hacker file. Her gaze drifting back to the name pwnst4r, she added, "And I think I may need to talk to Shannon as well. Could we set up a secure chat somewhere off the Cooper Security grid? Somewhere random and impossible to trace. Shannon knows how to do that, doesn't she?"

"I think so," Luke said, sounding uncertain. "How do I get back in touch with you? This number?"

"No, I'm burning this phone as soon as I hang up. I'll be in touch. This time I'll call Gabe. Tell him to be expecting the call." She hung up and handed the phone to Brand.

"Is Gabe one of the Coopers?"

"One of the fishing cousins," she answered with a half smile. "He's a former bass pro. Now he guides fishermen on Gossamer Lake."

"Sure you can trust him?"

"I'd trust any of the Coopers with my life."

Brand flashed a quick smile. "Are you sure about walking away from Cooper Security? You seem to be a big fan."

"They were great to me. They gave me opportunities to do a lot of good things for people in trouble, and I didn't have to answer to a bunch of bureaucrats to do it."

He grimaced a little at her words, but she didn't care. Brand might be a bureau man through and through, but she never had been part of that mind-set. She'd joined the FBI to do good things, and when she'd begun to understand the sometimes-ridiculous rules were more important to her superiors than the results, she'd decided she couldn't live under those strictures and look at herself in the mirror.

Brand might think his rejection of her had been the deciding factor, and maybe it had been the breaking point. But she'd already been thinking about leaving before Bluefield, West Virginia, ever happened.

And as much as it hurt to think about walking away from Adam Brand again, she'd do it if she had to. She'd spent the first seventeen years of her life imprisoned by her parents' bad choices.

Never again would she let someone else make her choices for her.

Not even Adam Brand.

Chapter Ten

The chat room was a temporary web address that Cooper Security's IT director, Shannon Stone, had set up. Cooper Security protocol was to give agents a way to interact with the head office covertly, without going through more obvious channels, so Shannon set up chat rooms as needed, then disabled them after each use, making it nearly impossible for intruders to use them to trick agents in the field. Gabe Cooper had called with a new chat-room address twenty minutes earlier, warning Delilah that if she wasn't on time, the room would disappear.

"You're on time," Brand grumbled in her ear as he looked at the chat-room window over her shoulder. "Where are they?"

Delilah was logged in under her Cooper Security code name, CDarling, a nickname Wade Cooper had given her the first time he'd heard her slip into her mountain drawl.

Brand had chuckled at the name, catching the meaning. "Charlene Darling? From *The Andy Griffith Show?*"

Grimacing, she'd nodded. "Apparently I have a hillbilly accent."

"No. Really?"

She had almost nudged him in the ribs before remembering he was still recovering from a bullet wound in the side.

Another name finally popped into the chat room: Leatherbrat. "That's Evie," she told Brand. "Her father is a retired Marine Corps general."

She typed in a greeting, using code that Evie would be able to interpret. Evie responded in kind, reassuring Delilah that she was talking to the real Evie Marsh Cooper.

"Where's g33kgrrl?" she typed, referring to Shannon.

"On her way. Last minute system blowup she had to tend to. What's up?" Evie asked.

Typing on the tablet's keyboard was unwieldy, making it harder to get her thoughts across in full, correctly spelled sentences. Delilah apologized in advance for any typos and outlined, in an abbreviated manner, their question about tracking down any holdings Wayne Cortland might have beyond the lumber mill in Travisville.

"I can do a full forensic search if you need me to," Evie offered. "Just give me the particulars."

Delilah had anticipated the question and had already pulled up the files on Cortland Lumber. She outlined what they knew and explained what they were looking for.

"So you think this is connected to what's going on with Davenport?" Evie asked.

"It must be, if he's the one behind the murders in Bitterwood, and we think he is."

"We?"

"Those of us still investigating the murders," she answered vaguely, giving herself a mental kick.

A third name popped up in the chat-room list, but it wasn't g33kgrrl. Instead, the name was Litehaus. Delilah's eyebrows rose. "Changed your handle?" she typed.

Litehaus, who Delilah assumed was Shannon, answered, "I'm a sentimental fool."

"Shannon and her husband have some thing about lighthouses," Delilah murmured to Brand. "I think there was one on the island where they met or something."

"Leather's catching me up on what you want," Shannon typed. "What do you need me for?"

"I'm looking into some hacktivists who may be involved in whatever Cortland's up to, and one of the names pinged my radar. I figured you're a computer geek, you might have heard of it. Someone named pwnst4r."

The other two remained silent so long Delilah feared she'd lost her connection to the chat room. "Hello?" she typed to test the theory. It showed up just fine.

"We're here," Shannon answered. "Where did you come across that name?"

Delilah exchanged a look with Brand.

"They know who it is," he murmured.

She nodded and typed in her answer. "I was looking into Adam Brand's disappearance and stumbled onto a list of notes he was making. Pwnst4r was one of the names he'd listed in a file of hacktivists he thought might be involved with whatever Cortland is up to."

There was another long moment of silence, as if the other two women were conferring on their side of the computer. Finally, Evie answered, "Neither of us is familiar with that name."

"They're lying," Delilah said flatly to Brand.

"I know."

"Okay," Delilah typed. "Thanks anyway."

"How do we get in touch with you if we need to?" Shannon asked.

"I'll be in touch through one of your cousins," Delilah answered and shut down her end of the chat room without waiting for a response.

"So that's it?" Brand asked. "They know who pwnst4r is but we let them get away without telling us?"

Delilah shook her head. "I know who pwnst4r is," she said.

Brand's brows lifted. "Who?"

"Ever heard of a code cracker named Endrex?"

Brand frowned. "The name's familiar...."

"It should be. He's the cracker who brought down the Espera Group last summer. He's the guy Jesse and Evie tracked down and saved to get the evidence against Morris Gamble and Katrina Hilliard." Gamble, the former U.S. Secretary of Energy, and Hilliard, who'd been President Cambridge's chief of staff, had both been indicted in a wide-ranging conspiracy to allow a multinational consortium called Espera Group to control and manipulate the production, sale and distribution of oil and natural-gas resources.

"I thought he went into witness protection," Brand said.

"I think he did. But if I know anything about Nolan Cavanaugh from my brief acquaintance with him, it's that he's too inquisitive for his own good. And he hates hacktivists—he thinks they're posers who have just enough skill to be dangerous and they often choose the wrong causes to champion." Delilah grinned, remembering the handful of visits she'd made to Nolan Cavanaugh while he was recuperating from his brush with death. "He's an iconoclast, but he's smart enough to generally know the good guys from the bad guys."

"So if he ran into these particular hacktivists and got wind of what they were up to—"

"—he might feel obligated to keep an eye on them and see if he could stop them," Delilah finished for him. "And he and Evie go way back—if she knows he's in witness protection, and she knows the online name he's using now, she'd protect him from anyone, including me."

"Surely she knows you're smart enough to see through it."

"I think that's what the long pauses were about," Delilah admitted. "Her way of telling me who it was without actually telling me. In case I'm under duress."

"Do they know I'm with you?"

Delilah looked up at Brand. "At this point, probably. All

this subterfuge wouldn't really be necessary, would it? I'd have just gone into a safe house with Seth and Rachel."

"Great." He grimaced.

"If they were going to turn you in, they'd have done it already," Delilah said flatly. "They're giving us a lot of rope."

"To hang ourselves."

"That's up to us, isn't it?"

"So how do we find this Nolan Cavanaugh if they don't help us?"

Delilah turned to face him, her pulse notching up as she realized how close he was sitting. She tried to hide her reaction. "I'll give that some thought. But in the meantime, I'm hungry. Think we can risk going out for real food?"

He rubbed his beard. "*Risk* is the right word."

"We could order takeout from a nice restaurant. Or do we need to conserve your money?"

"Actually, it wouldn't be a bad idea to go pick up that stash of supplies I told you about."

"Supplies? I thought it was just more money."

"It's both." He shot her a confident smile that made her blood run hot. "I like to be prepared."

"How prepared are we talking?"

He reached up and brushed a piece of hair behind her ear. "Boy Scout prepared, darlin'."

She lifted her chin and leveled her gaze with his. "You like playing with fire, Boy Scout?"

His blue eyes darkened. "Sometimes."

"Do you ever think about the scorched earth you leave behind?"

His gaze dropped to her mouth. "Not as much as I should," he admitted. He tried to pull his hand away from hers, but she held it firmly in her grip.

"Maybe you ought to." She lifted her other hand to his

face, allowing her fingers to tangle in his crisp beard. "Maybe you shouldn't start things you're not willing to finish."

He curled his free hand around the back of her neck, tugging her closer. "Who says I'm not willing to finish?"

A shock of desire jolted through her, settling like fire at her core. All these years later, she could remember how it felt to have him inside her, moving, surging, leaving her shuddering with release.

Wanting him so much now she could barely breathe.

"I always thought you were the most beautiful creature that ever walked into my life," he murmured, his breath hot against her cheek as he bent to whisper in her ear. "Sometimes you would walk into the office and I couldn't catch my breath."

She closed her eyes, drowning in memories. "You never showed it."

"I didn't dare." He tangled his fingers through her hair, snaring her in place. "I didn't dare let you see how much you affected me. Then I'd have been utterly lost."

"I thought you disapproved of me sometimes." Trembling as his lips brushed across her temple, she struggled to keep her head. "You were harder on me than on anyone else."

"I expected more from you," he corrected softly. "Because I knew you were brilliant and capable of so much more than anyone had ever challenged you to do."

To her surprise, tears burned her eyes at his words. She put her hand on his chest and pushed him away, turning her head so he couldn't see her reaction.

"Hammond?" He sounded puzzled as he bent toward her, trying to look into her eyes.

"We need to concentrate on finding Cavanaugh." Her voice came out ragged.

He caught her chin in his palm, making her look at him. A film of tears blurred his face, and she blinked rapidly, trying to drive them back. But a tear spilled down her cheek before she could stop it.

He caught the drop of moisture with the pad of his thumb, looking genuinely puzzled. "Did I say something to hurt you?"

"No." She tried to laugh, but the sound was watery and uncertain.

He laid his hands on her cheeks, studying her face. "You have to know you're brilliant and capable."

"I do know," she admitted with another little laugh. "But I've never heard anyone else say it."

He laughed in response, pressing his lips against her forehead. "I never knew you needed anyone to say it." He pulled away, smiling down at her. "You walked into my office like you owned the place and told me what you intended to do and how I was going to help you make it happen, remember?"

She nodded, cringing a little at the memory. "That's what you fancy educated people call *bravado.* I was scared out of my gourd but I didn't dare let anyone know it. So I pretended I was a big ol' bitch on wheels who wasn't going to let anyone tell me no. I kept hoping that if I did that long enough and loud enough, one day I might believe it myself."

"Did you?" He brushed back a piece of hair that clung to her damp cheek. "Believe it, I mean?"

"Yeah. Eventually." She pulled away from his grasp, needing room to breathe. Crossing to the motel-room window, she gazed out at the street beyond, where midmorning traffic was passing by with flashes of sunlight reflecting off windshields and chrome. She closed her eyes, watching bright bursts of colorful afterimages dance behind her eyelids. "Enough to know when it was time to walk away and start somewhere new."

Brand was silent behind her. Eventually, she opened her eyes and turned to look at him.

He gazed back at her with fathomless eyes. "I did what I had to do."

She managed a smile. "I know. So did I."

He looked away, his gaze falling on the tablet computer. "How do we find Nolan Cavanaugh?" he asked again.

She thought about the question, the answer popping into her head as if someone had dropped it from the ether. "We don't. We let him find us."

THOUGH THE DRIVE TO Hungry Mother Park, a Virginia state park nestled in the Blue Ridge Mountains, would have normally taken a little over an hour from Galax, Brand decided to play it safe and take back roads, adding almost an hour to the trip. But the payoff in scenery alone would have been worth the extra time. The added security of staying off the more highly traveled roads was almost an afterthought.

The snow that had hammered the Smokies had hit the mountains near the park as well, remnants visible in the higher elevations and even crusts of the white stuff lingering on patches of land hidden from more than an hour or two of direct sunlight. As a kid growing up on the Georgia coast, he'd have happily welcomed snowfall, but dealing with the icy precipitation during his years in D.C. had been enough to cure him of his childhood fascination.

Still, there was enough of the boy still left inside to find the sight of the snow-dusted mountains thrilling as Delilah drove the twisty road toward the park. As she neared the lake, he directed her to detour north on a less-traveled road that wound into the woodlands. She gave him a questioning look when, a few miles later, he told her to take a right onto a weed-eaten dirt road.

"I saw where you grew up," he murmured. "I know you know how to drive on roads like this."

She did as he asked, the Camaro jolting along the uneven

dirt track, sending him bouncing against his seat belt hard enough to jar his wounded side. He bit back a groan of pain and pointed to a grassy place well out of sight of the main road. "Park there. We'll hike the rest of the way."

Days of little sleep, combined with the bullet wound, had sapped much of his strength and made the uphill trek harder than he remembered. Delilah appeared to be full of restless energy, easily keeping pace with his longer legs and sometimes appearing to hold back to keep from rushing ahead.

The cold air and exercise flushed her cheeks with healthy pink, and he realized with surprise that he hadn't noticed until this moment that she hadn't been wearing makeup for days.

The hillbilly in her native habitat, he thought with a stifled grin, knowing she'd hate what he was thinking, even though he meant it as a heartfelt compliment. The Delilah Hammond he'd known eight years earlier had fought hard to wear a veneer of glamorous sophistication as if she came by it naturally, painting over her redneck roots with expensive cosmetics and a carefully chosen wardrobe that must have cost her a good chunk of her lower-level government salary.

It had taken him a few months to get a glimpse of the real woman beneath the polish. That was when the trouble really began for him. Because as tempting as the flashy facade of Agent Hammond had been, the real Delilah Hammond was downright irresistible.

"How much farther?" she asked as they reached a bend and the trail extended on as far as the eye could see.

"Right here," he answered, stopping at the base of a sprawling oak tree. He circled the tree and spotted the long, narrow green vinyl packet he'd left behind the tree trunk, hidden under a tangle of undergrowth.

"Is that the package?" Delilah asked, eyeing the small bundle with obvious skepticism.

He opened the bundle and pulled out a camp spade. "No, this is the tool to get us to the package." He started to put the spade in the dirt at the base of the tree when he spotted a tiny triangle of white sticking out of the earth. He froze in place, his heart suddenly slamming his ribs like a sledgehammer.

"What is it?" Delilah asked, going still in response to his reaction.

He looked around them, peering through the woods, the hair on the back of his neck prickling with warning.

"Someone's been here," he said.

Chapter Eleven

"Careful…" Delilah sucked in a deep breath as Brand cautiously shifted dirt away from the little plastic triangle sticking up from the dirt. "It might be booby-trapped."

"Yes, I know." He darted a quick look at her, not bothering to hide his frustration.

"Sorry." She winced as he touched the plastic. Nothing happened, so he gave a tug and a rectangle of plastic slipped free of the dirt.

"Hmm." Brand sat back on his heels and dusted crumbs of dirt away, holding up the object for a better look.

Bending closer, Delilah saw that the piece of plastic was about the size of a business card. Something was etched into the surface of one side. "What does that say?"

"'The Devonian Project,'" Brand read aloud.

"The what?"

Brand scanned the woods around them, as if he expected someone to step out from behind a tree and intone, Greek chorus–style, the meaning of the mystery. But the woods remained still and unhelpful.

"Someone left this here for a reason," he said finally, looking back at the patch of disturbed dirt at his feet.

"Do you think your supplies are still there?"

Brand picked up the camp shovel and started digging again. About six inches down, he uncovered the top of a black vinyl backpack. He gave a tug and the bag came free from the loosened dirt. Opening the flap, he checked inside.

"Well?"

"Everything seems to be here." Brand looked around again, a spooked expression on his face. "Let's get out of here."

He handed her the plastic rectangle and started hiking back toward the clearing where they'd left the Camaro.

By the time they reached the car, the darkening clouds that had been brewing in the west were overhead, thick and threatening. Fat drops of cold rain splatted against the windshield as Delilah stopped at the intersection with the main road, forcing her to engage the windshield wipers.

"Go right," Brand said.

She glanced at him. "Right?"

"Right takes us closer to Travisville."

"We're still going to Travisville after someone messed with your stuff?"

"Where else are we going to go?"

Squelching the urge to argue, she took a right onto the county road, while Brand opened the backpack and started digging through it.

"Don't suppose you have body armor and a rocket launcher in there?" Delilah said with a forced laugh.

"Sadly, no." Brand pulled out a cell phone and a wallet. "I do, however, have a new identity and a brand-new phone." He traded the wallet for his old one and put the old wallet and his old phone into the sack. "This will make it easy to check into a motel in Chilhowie."

"Is that where we're going?"

"For tonight. There are a couple of places we can stay there, and it's close enough to the interstate that we can make a fast exit if need be." Brand hooked the new phone up to an auto charger and plugged it into the cigarette-lighter socket to charge. "Unfortunately, I can't promise there'll be internet connections where we'll be staying, but there should be restaurants nearby with free Wi-Fi."

"Why does the word *Devonian* sound familiar to me?" she asked a few minutes of silence later.

"It's a geologic period," Brand answered. "I think it's called the Age of Fish, or something like that."

"So the Devonian Project would be about fish?"

Brand shot her a dubious look. "Since when did you ever think that literally, Hammond?"

"What I'm thinking is that I wish I was home with my computer and my internet and a nice hot cup of hazelnut coffee." She tamped down a shiver and turned up the Camaro's heater. "Then I could look up the Devonian Project in peace and comfort."

Brand reached across the narrow front seat and brushed the backs of his knuckles against her cheek. "I can't promise you your computer or even internet, but we'll stop for coffee in Chilhowie and find us somewhere that offers free internet so we can look it up. Just a few more minutes."

As it turned out, he was right. Within about ten minutes, they were driving through the small town of Chilhowie, searching for a restaurant with free Wi-Fi. They found a small fast-food burger joint with a sign in the window advertising free internet connection and pulled in.

"I'm going to be ten pounds heavier before this is over," Delilah grumbled as they entered the restaurant and lined up to order. They both opted for salad and settled at a small corner booth to eat and connect the tablet to the internet.

"The Devonian Project," Brand informed her a few minutes later, "appears to be a joint federal/private energy-research partnership." He met her curious gaze over the table. "And guess who the federal part is?"

It took a second for the obvious answer to click. "The Oak Ridge National Laboratory?"

"You always were my brightest agent," he murmured, the warmth in his voice making her toes curl in her sneakers. "It has something to do with exploiting oil-shale deposits in the Appalachian basin."

"Isn't that already being done?"

"Yes, but apparently this particular project is looking at areas that haven't yet been exploited because they've been considered low-yield. According to this website, the research partnership has found a way to increase the exploitable resources that can be reached by standard hydraulic fracturing."

"Fracking?" Delilah frowned. "That's a political hot potato. Might mean that the Oak Ridge National Laboratory really is somebody's target."

"I don't think Wayne Cortland is any sort of environmentalist. He runs a lumber mill."

"Yes, but that doesn't mean he wouldn't tap into someone else's passions, does it?"

Brand looked up at her. "Like our friendly neighborhood hacktivists?"

"Some of them lean toward social issues like environmentalism."

He nodded. "While militias tend to lean the opposite way."

"Not the most obvious of allies," Delilah said.

"But if you think about it, these militia groups are big on living off the land and very distrustful of government projects. This is a mission the hackers and the Blue Ridge Infantry can agree on."

"So what's in it for Cortland? How does he profit from siccing his crew on the Oak Ridge National Laboratory?"

Brand picked up the plastic card, running his finger over the words etched there. "That is the question, isn't it?"

THE BELLBRIDGE MOTEL was about as seedy a place as Brand had ever stayed in outside of a third-world country, but the bed didn't sag too much, and if there were stains on the bedding, they weren't immediately obvious. The Wi-Fi wasn't free and it wasn't entirely reliable, but it was the best they could hope for in such a place. Brand had paid the fee and considered himself lucky to have access to the internet at all.

Delilah set about cleaning the place up as well as she could while Brand sat down in one of the two rickety armchairs and started going through the portable document files they'd saved in a rush while they still had access to the restaurant's free Wi-Fi.

"As far as we know, Cortland doesn't own any of the land covered by the Devonian Project," he commented as he scanned one of the files. "So what's his interest?"

"You know what I'm wondering?" Delilah dropped the paper towel she'd been using to wipe down surfaces into the garbage can by the bed. "Who left you that cryptic little note? And is he a friend or a foe?"

"I think at the very least, an ally," Brand decided. "If he knew where to find my stash, he was clearly following me for a while. If he had wanted to stop me, he could have."

"If he's on your side, why didn't he leave a less cryptic message?"

"Maybe there's a reason he can't operate in the open." He looked up at her. "You and I know plenty of people who have to work in the shadows, for one reason or another."

With a sigh, she sat on the end of the bed. "I thought I was finally leaving all that cloak-and-dagger stuff behind."

"Is that really what you want?"

She met his curious gaze. "Yes. It is."

He felt a curling sensation in the center of his chest. He'd spent his whole adult life becoming very good at operating in the shadows if he needed to. He'd found a lot of excitement and satisfaction in working behind the scenes to keep a large, powerful nation safe from outside harm.

But there was a part of him, a growing part, that could almost understand Delilah's attitude.

Almost.

"You know, maybe we're approaching this whole thing from the wrong angle," Delilah said a few seconds later, examining the threadbare gray comforter covering the queen-size bed. "We're chasing after all the things we don't know about what Cortland is up to, but you know what we haven't given any real thought?"

He stretched his neck and stifled a yawn. He was tired, his injured side hurt and his head was beginning to ache. The last thing he needed was a quiz. "What haven't we given any real thought?"

"Why was Wayne Cortland so all-fired eager to get control of Davenport Trucking that he was willing to order people killed to make it happen?"

"It can't be the land he owns," Brand said flatly. "None of his land lies in any of the known oil-shale fields."

"Unless he owns land we don't know about," Delilah pointed out. "But that still doesn't explain his obsession with Davenport Trucking."

"Well, let's think about why anyone would want a trucking company."

"If he's part of the meth game, he might need trucks to haul supplies around. The government's cracked down hard on pseudoephedrine sales, so it can be hard to get your hands on enough of the raw materials for making meth."

"Hard, but not impossible."

"But how much easier would it be if you could truck it up from Mexico in your own fleet?"

"Okay, that's a possibility." Brand typed in a note on the

tablet. "But that doesn't explain what he's up to with the BRI or the anarchists."

"Well, we think he might actually be playing the BRI and the hacktivists for fools, right? Using their interest in stopping the Devonian Project for his own purposes."

"Right. But what purposes?"

"And we're back to figuring out how the Devonian Project could be at all connected to Davenport Trucking." Delilah scraped her hair back from her face with a frustrated jab. "I can't think."

"Me, either. It's been a long day. Maybe we should just sleep on it."

Delilah looked at her watch and rolled her eyes. "I'm not old enough—or young enough—to go to bed at seven-thirty."

Brand grinned. "Maybe we should see if we can find a movie on one of those cable stations the motel promised us and try to think about something else for a while."

Unfortunately, most of the stations the motel system carried came in snowy, wavery or both. They settled finally on a basketball game and Delilah scooted over so Brand could sit beside her on the bed, propping his head against the rickety headboard.

She squinted at the screen, which had started to roll. "Who's playing?"

"That looks like Kentucky blue."

She slumped back, not particularly interested. Closing her eyes, she let the murmur of the ambient crowd noises, along with the nonstop prattle of the announcers, lull her into a doze.

She heard a man's voice, speaking in a low, angry tone. It was a horribly familiar voice, one that had haunted her dreams long after it had fallen silent in real life.

"You's a stupid little bitch like your mama, ain'tcha, girl?"

She tried to close her ears to the sound of his voice, to the harsh mountain twang and the manic evil of it.

"Cain't even figure out a simple little puzzle. No wonder you washed out of that fancy FBI job."

"Shut up," she growled, putting her hands over her ears.

"It ain't the land that drives him. It's the access."

She dropped her hands from her ears. "Access?"

"Access is power."

She woke with a start.

"Hammond?" Brand's voice was practically in her ear, warm with concern.

"Access is power," she repeated aloud.

Brand stared at her. "What?"

She looked at him, her lips curving in a bleak smile. "Cortland doesn't own any land in the shale zone. But he owns a lot of land that would provide prime access to the Devonian Project's target fracking areas."

Brand's eyes narrowed. "Which could be claimed by eminent domain."

"Exactly. But only if the Devonian Project gets the green light."

"So Cortland's not trying to get in on the fracking boom in his neck of the woods."

"He's trying to stop it."

Brand rubbed his beard. "How does that explain why he went after Davenport Trucking?"

"Because they have a connection to the Oak Ridge National Laboratory." Delilah smiled grimly as more pieces of the puzzle began to click into place. "I saw it on the public-relations section of the Davenport Trucking website a few weeks back, when I was trying to figure out what Paul Bailey had been up to. They sold the lab the trucks they've been using to haul equipment between the ORNL and some off-site research partners. They also have a service contract with Oak Ridge."

Brand's eyes widened. "Which means—"

"Which means if you wanted to get a truck into Oak Ridge without raising an eyebrow, using a Davenport Trucking vehicle would be a damned good way to do it."

Chapter Twelve

"Do you think he's already located a different trucking company to exploit?" Delilah's voice stole quietly into the darkness of the motel room.

Brand opened his eyes. "I thought you were going to get some shut-eye."

"My brain won't turn off."

His brain was going ninety miles an hour, too. "I don't know. I'd have to do some research to figure out if there were other trucking companies with contracts with Oak Ridge."

She made a growling noise low in her throat, a familiar sound that made Brand smile at the darkness. When she was frustrated, she sounded like a feral cat. "How can we just lie here and pretend Wayne Cortland's not out there planning to do God knows what to a nuclear laboratory?"

"We're trying to get some sleep so we'll be fresh and alert in the morning," he reminded her.

"It's not working."

"Hammond—"

"What if he's given up on the direct attack? What if he's going to try to cripple Oak Ridge another way?"

"How can we even be sure crippling Oak Ridge is what he wants?"

"I've been thinking about that, too," Delilah said. The bed shifted beside Brand as she turned, propping herself on one elbow. He rolled his head to the side and met her gaze in the dim light filtering in from outside the motel window. "It's just too big a coincidence that Davenport has a service contract with the Oak Ridge National Laboratory. No way that doesn't mean anything. So I figure Cortland's attempt to take over control of Davenport Trucking was all about that contract and the access it would give him to the laboratory."

"I'd tend to agree," Brand said, trying not to notice how warm and sweet she smelled lying there in the bed beside him.

"And the point of getting access to the laboratory would be one of maybe three things. Stealing something from the laboratory, delivering something to the laboratory or doing something to the laboratory. Right?"

"Right."

"I don't see what they could steal from the laboratory that would enable Cortland to stop the Devonian Project. Any research being done at the laboratory can probably be replicated easily enough. Most labs have redundant systems in place in case of accidents."

"True. And I'm not sure how delivering something there makes any sense, unless it was a bomb or something."

"Which leads to point three—doing something to the laboratory."

"But how does doing something to the laboratory help stop the Devonian Project?" Brand asked, although he was starting to see the outlines of a plot taking shape.

"It's a nuclear laboratory. Even a small, nonnuclear incident there might be enough to sway public opinion away from allowing fracking so close to the lab and other nuclear facilities. Three Mile Island's partial meltdown happened in 1979 and people still talk about it."

"So," Brand added, beginning to see the bigger picture, "if

Cortland can't get his hands on the trucking company, he'll need another way to attack the lab and cause an incident."

"And I've been pondering that, too." Delilah shifted positions, rolling closer to Brand until her hip nestled next to his. "What if those hacktivists Cortland's been grooming can find a way to infiltrate the computer system at Oak Ridge and create an incident?"

"Surely those systems are hardened against cyberattack," Brand argued, although not without doubt. More than one supposedly hardened computer system had proved vulnerable to outside attack over the years. It was a source of constant, if well-hidden, concern among the government agencies tasked with protecting the country from outside threats.

"Probably, but it would take just one little unanticipated breach to cause a big mess. If hackers found a way in, they'd be certain to trumpet their success, and there's no way Oak Ridge could cover up the breach, even if they got it swiftly under control. All it would take would be for Cortland to whisper a few concerned questions in the right ears about the safety of fracking so close to nuclear facilities that clearly aren't able to provide foolproof security even for their own computer systems—"

"The press would eat it up." Brand grimaced. "And Cortland's empire remains undisturbed, free to continue making money off people's addictions."

"And whatever other crimes they're up to over there in Travisville." Delilah rolled off the mattress and circled around to the tablet computer Brand had left lying on the table next to the bed.

"What are you doing?" Brand asked.

"Banking on the idea that Nolan Cavanaugh is a night owl."

With a weary groan, Brand sat up, grimacing against the stab of pain in his side. Over Delilah's shoulder, he saw she had opened a chat-room window, similar to the one they'd used earlier with Evie Cooper and Shannon Stone. There was one name in the chat participants list: friendofleatherbrat. "Is that you?" he asked.

She nodded. "Last year, Evie got in touch with Nolan Cavanaugh using this chat room. It was one they'd used in the past, years ago. Apparently Cavanaugh was still monitoring the chat room and knew when she entered it to talk to him, even though they hadn't used the room in years."

Brand looked at the chat list. Delilah's handle remained alone. "Looks like he's not biting this time."

Almost before he'd finished the sentence, another name popped up on the chat list—"Phreakwrld."

"Hmm," Delilah said.

"Not who you were expecting?"

"Maybe he's using an alias."

"They're all aliases."

"You know what I mean." Delilah typed a message into the chat window. "Did you almost blow up in a gas explosion last fall?"

Brand swallowed a snort of laughter. "Not much for conversational foreplay, huh? Just get right down to business."

She shot him a glare that sent an electric shock of desire straight through to his sex.

"Who are you?" Phreakwrld asked.

"A friend of Leatherbrat. Used to work with her. I'm looking for her friend pwnst4r."

There was a long pause before the other chatter answered, "You don't know pwnst4r."

"Leatherbrat does. And if you're who I think you are, we've actually met before. In a Birmingham hospital. You called me Legs."

Phreakwrld's next answer was a profanity.

"Legs?" Brand asked.

"I was wearing a pair of skinny jeans. Made my legs look damned good, if I do say so myself." She typed in a new question. "So, can we cut the crap? Are you now pwnst4r? Because if you are, I need your help."

After a pause, Phreakwrld disappeared.

"Well, hell," Brand said.

"Wait a minute," Delilah murmured, bending closer to the tablet as if she could will Phreakwrld into reappearing. After a long, tense moment, another name appeared in the chat list.

Pwnst4r.

Brand muttered a profanity.

"I hear you left the company," pwnst4r typed.

"What did he do, call Evie while he was out of the chat?" Brand asked.

"Maybe." Delilah typed her answer. "I did. But I need help, and I think you and I might be after the same thing."

"What's that?" pwnst4r asked.

"Stopping Wayne Cortland," Delilah answered.

There was another long pause that made Brand's heart beat a little faster. "Do you think there's a chance he's working for Cortland and not the feds?"

"I can only tell you he put his life at risk to stop some very bad men last year. I can't see him switching sides easily, and there's nothing you've told me about Wayne Cortland that would inspire any loyalty from a man like Nolan Cavanaugh."

A new message popped into the chat window. "DoS attack on SCADA, ORNL. Trust no one. Not even the NRC."

Then pwnst4r disappeared from the chat room. And though Brand and Delilah waited almost ten minutes, he didn't reappear.

"I don't think he's going to tell us anything more than that," Delilah said with a frown, closing the chat-room window.

Brand reached around her and picked up the tablet. "To

be safe, let's purge the cache and the history." He set about doing so while Delilah stretched in the chair, giving him a far-too-tempting view of her slender curves on display beneath the Virginia Tech T-shirt and soft cotton exercise pants she wore as pajamas.

"'Not even the NRC,'" she quoted. "Nuclear Research Council?"

"Probably," Brand agreed.

"Which means what? He thinks someone in the NRC is in Cortland's pocket?"

"Last year, the Secretary of Energy and the president's chief of staff were busted for helping Espera Group plot against its opponents. You really think someone in the NRC is any less vulnerable to corruption than those two?"

She sighed. "I guess not."

Brand put his hands on her shoulders, gently kneading the knots of tension he felt there. She flinched at his touch, then relaxed, actually leaning back toward him as he gave her muscles a light massage. "There's not a damned thing we can do about any of this before morning, Hammond. Try to let it go. Get in bed and let's get some sleep."

She shook her head. "I've got to find out what SCADA is."

"Supervisory Control and Data Acquisition," he answered.

She looked over her shoulder at him. "Nerd."

He grinned. "It's basically how big plants, such as power companies or gas companies—or nuclear reactors—monitor and control all functions of the plant from one central location."

"I know what a DoS attack is—denial of service. I presume a DoS attack on the SCADA at Oak Ridge would be a very bad thing."

"If they throw enough external communication requests at the SCADA system, it could cause an overload and disrupt the normal communications necessary to make the systems work properly. That could be disastrous. But Oak Ridge and other nuclear plants have been hardening their systems against those kinds of attacks for a while now."

"But stuff gets through," Delilah said with a grimace. "We hear about failures all the time—hackers stealing thousands and thousands of credit-card numbers, or taking over government websites—"

"I think that's what Nolan Cavanaugh may be doing in the middle of this. He knows how hackers work. He lives in that same world, even if it's in the more legitimate part."

"Takes a hacker to stop a hacker?"

"The FBI has hired many a reformed hacker over the years."

"You think Cavanaugh's working for the FBI?"

"Probably. If not the FBI, then some other alphabet agency."

Delilah turned around in the chair, facing him. She looked sleepy and frustrated. "It feels like time is running out for us, doesn't it?"

He couldn't stop himself from touching her face, letting his fingers slide lightly across the curve of her jaw. "Not yet. We're not through fighting, are we?"

Her dark eyes softened as they met his. "*We.* It's been a long time since you and I have been a we, hasn't it?"

"Yes." He smiled at the thought. "We were always a pretty good we, though, weren't we?"

She laughed. "We may be a pretty good we, but we do terrible things to the English language when we're exhausted." She reached her hands out to him. He caught them and she pulled herself to her feet.

But she didn't let go of his hands, standing over him with a half smile curving her lips. "When I joined the FBI, I told myself I was going to be there until retirement. I had this whole big plan for how I'd rise in the ranks and eventually become the director. I figured I could learn to schmooze with the political class and make myself indispensable to some future president."

"You'd have had some future president eating out of your hand," he agreed, smiling up at her.

Her own smile faded slowly. "Water under the bridge." She gave a little tug of her hands, but he held on.

"Why did you leave? *Was* it because of me?" he asked.

She shook her head. "That was a catalyst, but it wasn't the reason."

"I never meant for you to leave. I believed in you as an agent. I wanted you to have every opportunity to go as far in the bureau as you wanted to go." He caressed the back of her hand with his thumb. "I didn't want to be the reason you didn't."

Her eyes narrowed. "And you didn't want me to be the reason you didn't go as far as you could."

He felt a flutter of conviction. She was right. He had thought of his own career as much as hers. Maybe more. And look where it had gotten him. He was on the run, risking everything to prove to an ever-skeptical bureaucracy that he was a truthful, honorable man.

The FBI didn't believe him.

But Delilah had. Without question. Eight years of separation and unspoken hurt hadn't changed her faith in him, in the kind of man he was.

He didn't deserve her. But God help him, he was beginning to think he'd never be happy without her. "I handled everything so badly."

"I don't know that there was a way to handle it well," she murmured, her eyelashes dropping to hide her dark eyes. "I knew when we locked the bedroom door that night in West Virginia that there wasn't going to be a happy ending for us. I guess I just thought we could make it last a little longer than it did."

"You don't believe in happy endings."

She looked up at him then, her dark eyes blazing with old pain. "Do *you?* Really?"

"I do. I just don't think everyone gets to find them."

"Less bleak than my worldview, I suppose." Her lips quirked. "I've learned not to have any illusions. It makes the world more palatable."

He released her hands, expecting her to walk away. But she remained in front of him, gazing at him from beneath the fall of dark hair spilling across her cheeks.

She touched his face, her fingers rasping against his thickening beard. "So scruffy. Not at all like the Adam Brand I knew."

"I'm different from that man in a lot of ways," he said, realizing with a rush of emotion that he was telling the truth. He'd spent eight years without her, trying to pretend his life was on its proper track and that nothing had really changed with her absence. But it had taken just a few days having her back in his life to know that the previous years had been a farce.

He wasn't the same man. He wasn't sure he even wanted to be that man anymore. Not if it meant watching her walk out of his life again.

But she was different, too. Less hopeful. Less naive.

So much more desirable, if that was possible. But even less attainable than before, though there were no professional obstacles standing in the way.

"I want you," she whispered, bending to touch her mouth to his.

An electric shock zapped through him at that light, simple brush of her lips, zigzagging its way through his chest into his groin. He trembled, trying to be still, to let her lead, afraid to do or say anything that might drive her away from him again, this time for good.

She drew away an inch, just enough to speak with a whisper of breath against his cheek. "I have no expectations."

"You should." He lifted his hands to her waist, his fingers sliding beneath the hem of her T-shirt until they brushed against the silken heat of her skin. "You should expect adoration. Slavish worship."

She laughed softly. "I'd settle for slavish foot rubs."

He tightened his grip on her waist and tugged her on the bed next to him, eliciting a little bark of surprised laughter from her. He caught her legs and pulled them into his lap. "Your wish is my command."

He plucked off her thick cotton socks, baring her long, narrow feet. Her toenails, he noted with a smile, were painted a bright, shocking blue. "You rebel," he murmured, pressing his thumb into the pad of her foot.

She groaned with pleasure. "If I'd known you were so good at this, I might have stuck around a little longer eight years ago."

He ran his hand up her ankle and beneath the cotton trousers to stroke her calf. "If only I'd known it was a selling point."

Her back arched a little as he reached a sensitive area behind her knee. "Brand, I know I started this—"

"But you're having second thoughts?"

"Well, I don't have any protection, for one thing." She looked at him, regret in her dark eyes.

"I do."

One of her dark eyebrows rose. "You normally bring condoms on the run with you?"

He smiled. "No. But when I saw a box hanging near the cash register at that last place we stopped for gas, I bought some."

"Should I find that flattering?"

"You should." He tickled the back of her knee, making her squirm a little. "I'm not being presumptuous, mind you."

"But, being the Boy Scout that you are, you like to be prepared?"

He grinned. "Exactly."

She pulled her legs out of his lap and launched herself at him, driving him back into the bed pillows. Twining her fingers with his, she pinned his arms above his head and straddled his hips. "Weren't prepared for that, were you?"

"No, but I can't complain." He shifted beneath her so that his growing hardness pressed firmly against the softness of her sex. "Nope, no complaints."

She bent to nip the underside of his jaw. "You are a wicked, wicked man, Agent Brand."

He turned his face until he captured her mouth with his. Her lips parted, her warm breath spilling into his mouth as her tongue sought his. Desire coursing through his blood like fire, he flipped her onto her back, pinning her beneath him as he kissed her deeply, thoroughly, desperate to brand her with his passion before fate found another way to rip her from him.

He forced himself to draw away, to look into her dark eyes and ask the question he dreaded to ask but knew he must. "I can't promise you anything. I don't know how any of this will end. So are you sure you really want this?"

Her eyes blazed up at him, full of heat and intent. "No expectations, remember?"

"None?" he asked, his tone teasing as he lowered his mouth to the fluttering vein in her neck. He nipped the skin, then soothed it with his tongue. "No expectations at all?"

"Well," she said, the word ending in a gasp, "maybe one or two."

"I'll keep that in mind," he said, lowering his mouth to hers again.

Chapter Thirteen

Their first tie together had been early January, just a few weeks after Christmas, in a bed-and-breakfast in Bluefield, West Virginia. Delilah would normally have been on the undercover assignment with one of the younger agents, her usual partner in most assignments that required a man and a woman to present themselves as lovers. His name had been Jim Fielding, and he'd been her first real friend in Washington, D.C., taking her under his wing when she joined the task force.

"Have you heard from Ella recently?" she murmured aloud in the dark, quiet aftermath of their lovemaking.

"Not in a couple of years." Brand's voice rumbled beneath her ear. "She sent a picture of Jim Junior at his first baseball game. He looks so much like his dad."

Old grief stabbed her in the heart. "It's so wrong that he's not there to see it."

"I know."

Jim Fielding had died a week before the assignment was supposed to start, gunned down outside a convenience store in Arlington where he'd stopped to pick up diapers on his way home to his wife and new baby. Brand had postponed the sting operation, meant to draw out a serial arsonist who'd been targeting bed-and-breakfasts in West Virginia, eastern

Kentucky and the southeastern corner of Virginia—finding Jim's murderer had taken precedence.

In the end, it had been nothing but a case of Jim Fielding being in the wrong place at the wrong time, getting out of his car to go into the store just as the robbers were coming out after killing the clerk. He hadn't even had time to pull his weapon before they shot him three times in the chest and head. He'd been dead before he hit the ground.

"Why did you take Jim's place on that sting?" she asked, letting her fingers play along the path of dark hair that grew down the center of his abdomen. "You could have assigned one of the other men on the task force."

"I knew you were still grieving Jim. We all were, but I knew you'd felt it the hardest."

"Because I'm a woman?" She looked up at him, wondering how much her sex had played into his decision. Had he seen her as weaker because she was female? He'd never seemed to try to protect her from dangerous situations just because she was a woman, but he also never went on undercover assignments for the task force, preferring to stick to the supervisory role, the man behind the curtain pulling all the strings.

"Because you and Jim were best friends, and I knew losing him hit you like a freight train."

True, she thought. It had. She'd grieved for him as deeply as if he'd been family. Maybe, in a way, she'd allowed Jim to take the place of Seth, the brother she'd loved but couldn't save from the life he'd chosen.

"You wanted to make sure I didn't let my sadness show?" She'd worked hard during the assignment to hide her lingering pain, to show the world only a vibrant, passionate woman in love with the man who shared her bed in the honeymoon suite. She'd even kept up appearances with Brand when they were alone, desperate to prove herself as a competent agent who could work through the grief.

"I knew you wouldn't let it show." There was warmth in his voice, and she looked up to find him smiling. "You would've died before you let it show on the job."

"I did let it show, though."

"Not on the clock." He stroked her hair, dropping a kiss on her temple. "When the snowstorm hit and we couldn't get any transportation out, we weren't on the clock anymore. What happened that night was the two of us letting go, releasing all that pent-up emotion."

"Grief sex?"

"Partially, yeah." He tipped her chin up, making her look at him. "You know that was part of it."

She nodded. "But not all of it."

He laid his head back on the pillow. "No, not all of it."

"You were playing with fire, assigning yourself to play my lover." She hadn't understood at first what drove him all those years ago. She'd been shocked when he'd told her his plans, confused and worried that he didn't think she was capable of doing the job without his direct supervision.

But that night in snowy West Virginia, when he'd seduced her with masterful skill and determination, she'd begun to understand that he was anything but indifferent to her. That his reserve, those moments when he'd seemed determined to keep his distance, had been more about preserving his own control than any lack of attraction to her.

"I spent so much time trying to make you react to me. I almost couldn't believe it when you did."

"I worked damned hard not to react to you." He brushed a lock of her hair back, giving him a better look at her face in the dim morning light. "I didn't want you to keep getting away with your femme-fatale act."

She blushed at the memory. "I did lay it on a little thick."

Propping his head on his hand, he used the other hand to draw maddening circles along the ridge of her collarbone.

"You knew you were attractive, and you used it as a bludgeon."

"Bludgeon?" She shot him a look. "Rapier, maybe."

"Felt like a bludgeon," he said with a slight smile. "Right between my eyes. You had most of the agents in our section salivating to be near you."

"I couldn't be the smartest or the strongest or the most experienced," she murmured. "But I could be the sexiest."

"That you were." His fingertips lingered along the tendon in the side of her neck. "But you were stronger and smarter than you believed."

"I was so attracted to you," she confessed. "And you didn't give me anything to work with."

"I wasn't going to be handled by a green agent, no matter how sexy she was." He caught her hand, drawing her knuckles to his lips. "And I wanted you to be careful. People in bureaucracies talk. And a few exaggerated stories could ruin an agent's chances of reaching the top."

"You were protecting my virtue?" She shot him another look.

"Your reputation, maybe." He sounded unapologetic. "I knew you didn't sleep your way onto the task force, because I know the good work you did to get there. But there were plenty of jealous agents who'd have been happy to spread rumors that could knock you back down the ladder where they thought you belonged."

"And then you slept with me, and all that concern went out the window?" she teased.

"No. Not out the window. It seemed more important than ever to protect your professional reputation."

"Is that why you cut me off completely?"

He rolled over onto his back again, gazing up at the ceiling. "No."

She rolled on her back as well, closing her eyes. "I didn't think so."

"A relationship with you couldn't happen. Not with both of us on the task force. One of us would have had to leave, and I didn't want that to happen. I valued your work too much to send you to another section, and I had no intention of asking for a transfer for myself."

"And then I resigned from the FBI and ruined all your plans."

"Yeah. I really didn't anticipate that happening."

"Because you thought you had it all under control." She turned to look at him again. Rosy dawn light seeped through the narrow gap in the curtains, falling across his profile. He was really a beautiful man, she thought, admiring the straight line of his nose, the firm curve of his mouth, the shadowy contours of his lean cheeks and cleft chin beneath the beard's shadow. A beautiful, frustrating man. "You can't control everything in your life. Especially other people."

"As I've learned the hard way." His voice was a low grumble.

"Would you have done things differently if you'd known how it would turn out?"

He turned his head, meeting her gaze. "Back then? No. I wouldn't have. I wasn't going to leave my position with the task force, and I wouldn't have tried to have a secret relationship with you. It would have been too dangerous and you'd have been the one who got hurt the most, not me."

"Altruistic of you."

"No. I was thinking of my own career as well."

"What about now?"

"I don't know," he answered after a brief pause. "My life is out of control, and I don't know if or when I'll ever get back all the things I've lost in the past few months."

"You will. We're going to find the truth, and you'll be cleared."

"Maybe. Probably, now that you're on my side." He touched her face briefly, then dropped his hand back to his side. "But I have no idea what happens after that."

"I don't know, either." She smiled a little sheepishly. "Considering how much I used to hate even thinking about Smoky Ridge, I can barely believe I've returned to the mountains voluntarily. But I did, and I intend to stay. My brother's there, and he's finally made the changes to his life that I've been wanting for so long. My mom's trying, God bless her, to stop drinking and make a little something of her life, too. She's still young enough to have some good years left if she can make it this time. I can't walk away from that, not to go back to D.C. and that life. It's not what I want anymore. I'm not sure now it ever really was."

"So we're at an impasse, then, aren't we?"

"I guess we are." She looked away, afraid the tears suddenly stinging the backs of her eyes might spill. She'd already cried in front of Brand once. She didn't want to do it again.

She didn't even know why she felt like crying. She'd known, eight years ago, that things would never work out between her and Brand. Relationships were difficult in the best of circumstances, and Delilah knew her own past had scarred her to the point that having a long-term, healthy relationship was probably never going to happen for her. She'd grown up in the heart of dysfunction, in the poverty and desperation of life on Smoky Ridge. People from Smoky Ridge didn't get happily ever afters. Another manifestation of the Smoky Ridge curse.

Of course, she'd thought her brother was an even worse prospect for happily ever after, but he and Rachel were showing all the signs of two people who fully intended to give wedding bells and gold bands a chance.

And her old pal Sutton Calhoun, the most confirmed bachelor she knew, had recently asked Bitterwood police detective Ivy Hawkins to marry him. Of course, Ivy had said yes—the scrappy little hillbilly had been in love with Sutton since they were all kids.

So, okay, maybe the Smoky Ridge curse wasn't as all-encompassing as she'd thought. But it didn't mean she was going to be one of the lucky few who evaded its effects. So far her track record was pretty bad.

"Hammond?"

She blinked back the last sting of tears and answered. "Yeah?"

"How sure are you that Nolan Cavanaugh can be trusted?"

"Evie trusts him, and she's pretty levelheaded."

"I didn't ask how sure Evie Cooper was. I asked how sure you are."

She rolled to her side again to look at him. He still lay relaxed on his back, but his face was turned toward her, and his gaze was serious. "I don't know him well enough to be certain of anything."

He gave a slow nod. "Let's get dressed and get out of here."

She frowned as he sat up and reached for the clothes he'd discarded earlier. "You think he's got a way to locate us? How?"

"I don't know. Maybe there's some way to pinpoint an IP address through that chat room. I'm not technologically savvy enough to know for sure. But if we're wrong, and he's working with the hacktivists and not against them, it won't be hard to pinpoint this motel's IP address and figure out where we are."

She forced herself up from the bed. "I'm not leaving here without a shower."

"Agreed." He dropped the clothes on the bed without putting them on and headed for the bathroom. He stopped in the door. "You coming?"

She stared back at him. "You want us to shower together?"

"Faster that way." His eyebrows notched up. "Can't handle it, Hammond?"

Jutting her chin, she strode across the room, trying to forget that she was stark naked and about eight years older than the last time she'd bared her body to him. "We'll see who can't handle it, big guy."

His eyes gleamed with masculine appreciation as she joined him in the shower, making her glad she'd stuck to a regular workout routine in the Cooper Security gym.

Though it was a struggle, she managed to keep her mind on the need for speed rather than how bloody amazing Brand's slick, naked body looked for a man in his forties. She checked his wound while they showered, pleased and relieved to see that it was healing at a fast clip. He'd managed to avoid a major infection, which was a minor miracle, and when she helped him bandage it later while they were dressing, he admitted it barely hurt at all anymore.

"You must keep yourself in good shape," she murmured as she patted down the last piece of tape.

He gave her a warm, appreciative look. "So do you."

She gave him a warning look. "If you want me to stay focused on the danger we're in, stop trying to distract me."

"I'll drive. I've had more sleep than you have." He pulled on his shirt and topped it with a thick leather jacket he'd stashed in the backpack they'd dug up from the woods near Hungry Mother State Park.

"Where are we off to next?"

"There's a cabin south of Abingdon, about halfway between there and Travisville. It belonged to Liz, but it's registered under her grandmother's name. It's not likely anyone outside her immediate family would know about it, and Liz was the only one who ever used it."

Delilah felt a flutter of jealousy. "You and she went there together?"

"Only once. And it was after we broke things off. We just stopped there to pick up some things she wanted to take back to her apartment."

"Oh."

He touched her face. "A little jealous?"

"No." At his skeptical look, she grimaced. "Okay, yes. A little. But I'll get over it."

He gave her cheek one more stroke, then turned to finish packing. She already had her duffel bag packed and ready to go, so they took a final look around the room to make sure they'd forgotten nothing and headed out to the Camaro. While she stashed their things in the back, he went to the motel's front office and settled up the bill with the night clerk.

"What did you tell him about why we're leaving early?" she asked when he slid behind the wheel of the Camaro.

"Family emergency." He slanted a look at her that made her toes curl. Of course, she had a feeling he could have made a silly face at her and her toes would have curled. She'd completely lost control of her emotions where Brand was concerned.

There was no way any of this could end well, even if they managed to catch Cortland red-handed with his finger in every cookie jar in the Appalachian Mountains.

"I've been thinking about what to do next," she said a few minutes later, after they'd headed west on I-81, toward Abingdon.

Brand glanced away from the road. "Yeah?"

"I think I need to approach him directly."

"No."

"Hear me out."

"No," Brand said more vehemently. "I wouldn't have sent you for a face-to-face if we were still in the FBI, and I sure as hell won't do it without any backup at all."

"Listen, Brand—he wants to get his hands on you. Either to turn you in to the FBI or, more likely, to get rid of you himself so you'll stop being such a damned nuisance. I can give him what he wants. I can give him you."

Brand shot another look her way. "How?"

"Well, I won't really give him you, obviously, but Cortland doesn't have to know that. I have a history with you—a troubled one—and you know what they say about hell's fury and women scorned."

He was silent for a moment before he murmured, "Go on."

"I contact Cortland. Set up a meeting—I know where you are and I'm ready to turn you in."

"Why would you turn me in after you've been helping me?"

"Because once again, you slept with me and then dumped me after you had your way. I was foolish enough to think that this time you'd changed. That you were sincere about wanting to be with me."

Brand grimaced.

"Now I want revenge."

He slanted a quick look at her. "Do you?"

"What?"

"Want revenge?"

He was serious, she realized. She turned in the seat to face him. "Brand, I know things are complicated, and I went into this situation with both eyes open. If I live to regret it, it won't be your fault. It'll be mine."

"I don't want you to regret it."

"Maybe I won't." She didn't sound confident, even to her own ears, but Brand didn't comment.

A few moments later, he said, "You can't trust Cortland. There's no way to be certain he won't kill you on sight."

"But I'll be offering him something he wants a lot worse than killing me," she argued. "He'll hear me out."

"And then what?"

"I'll be wired."

"No." He shook his head. "That'll be the first thing he looks for."

"We can set up something really high-tech. We know the stuff to get. Maybe a button mike with a remote receiver. He'd never spot it."

"This is my mess, Delilah, not yours."

She stared at him, frustrated. "You called me Delilah."

"It's your name."

"You only call me Delilah when you're putting your foot down."

"It's too dangerous."

"I'm a trained agent. I'm way more trained than I was eight years ago when I was working with you." She leaned toward him, catching a whiff of the shower gel they'd used just an hour earlier. It reminded her of how they'd spent the evening, how it had felt to be in his arms again, after all this time. The feel of him surging inside her, as relentless as the tide, and how much harder it was going to be to let him go again after allowing herself a taste of what she'd lost before.

What she was suggesting would bring an end to their time together, one way or another. While part of her wondered why she was in a hurry to bring that end about, the other part knew, with grim certainty, that there'd be pain no matter when things ended. Better, perhaps, to end their ill-fated reunion quickly and get on with the bleeding.

Time was running out. Brand couldn't stay on the run forever, and she had a new job waiting for her in Bitterwood. Her mother was in the middle of another attempt to dry out and change her life, and Delilah should be there for her instead of chasing around the countryside with Brand.

"I'm going to do it, with or without you," she said bluntly, her tone designed to allow no further argument. "I'd rather have you at my back, but that's up to you."

Brand's mouth flattened to a thin line, and she could see in the tense set of his muscles that he was furious with her ultimatum. But she knew he'd never leave her to handle the confrontation alone. If there was one thing she could depend on, it was that Adam Brand would never leave a man—or woman—in the field to fend for herself.

"I'm in," he said.

She smiled. "Never doubted it for a moment."

Chapter Fourteen

Perspiration glistened on Delilah's bare skin, giving her an ethereal glow in the warm light of breaking dawn. She had always been a beautiful creature, but age had given her beauty depth. She looked like a goddess, Brand thought, watching her breasts rise and fall as she struggled to regain her breath. A glowing, glorious goddess.

He felt boneless himself, utterly sated by their lovemaking. It had been a long time since he'd been willing—or able—to set aside pressing worries in favor of slaking his desire, but Delilah had always brought out that need in him. He'd thought it dangerous to be so vulnerable to someone with the power to derail his focus, but in this moment, his body still trembling with pleasure, he realized her effect on him was a treasure.

Being with her had given him a sense of peace, a feeling of hope at a moment when he'd begun to fear there was no way out of the mess he was in. Just as their one night together eight years ago had given him hope after the loss of one of his best agents had made him doubt his ability to continue sending men and women into danger when there was no way to be certain they'd come back alive.

How was he supposed to let her go again when all this was over?

Delilah rolled over and propped her head on her hand,

smiling at him like a kitten that had just discovered a jug of cream. "That was worth delaying sleep for."

"You may not think so later today when we're trying to stay awake long enough to set up our sting."

She ran her hand down his chest, her fingers tangling in his hair. "I don't think so."

He caught her hand, entwining his fingers with hers. "You know, we could just forget all about that and keep doing this all day."

"Wicked man." She bent and kissed him, a slow, deep, wet kiss that sparked a fire low in his belly. She pulled away, breathless. "We agreed about this plan."

"You stated what you were going to do and told me it was your way or the highway." He let go of her hand so he could trace the tempting curve of her slender waist. Letting his hand slide lower to cover her backside, he tugged her closer, until their bodies were flush.

"Oh," she said, her eyes widening as his erection pressed against her lower belly. "You're an impressive man, Agent Brand."

He rolled onto his back, pulling her with him. She settled over him, her hair spilling over her shoulders in a dark curtain. "You're so beautiful."

She laughed. "I bet you say that to all the naked women who straddle you."

"I don't," he told her as she shifted closer to where he needed her to be.

She bent to kiss him, her hot tongue sliding over his. "Thank you."

He reached across to the bedside table for another condom before he lost the ability to think.

THEY WOKE A few hours later, took a shower together and prepared a lunch of soup and sandwiches in the cabin's small kitchen. A gas-powered generator outside provided enough electricity to run the small refrigerator, where they'd stashed the bag of cold cuts and bottles of water they'd bought at a twenty-four-hour convenience store on their way to the cabin. Luckily, Brand also knew how to turn on the gas to run the old stove to heat up the soup.

"When this is over, I'll settle up the bill," he said, even though she hadn't asked.

"I know." She knew he would do whatever he could to make things right, to repair any damage he'd done in trying to save his own life and reputation. It was the kind of man he was.

"There's a spy shop in a little town called Blakeville, just south of Abingdon. Tech Palace. Tiny place, but they're well stocked with a lot of cool gadgets. And they don't ask a lot of nosy questions."

"I've got my cover story figured out anyway," Delilah told him. "I'm being stalked by an ex-boyfriend and the cops won't listen to me. So I want to record him harassing me without his knowing it. Virginia is a one-party consent state, so that should pass the smell test."

"Good story. Simple and believable." He pulled his money clip out, peeled off three hundred dollars and handed her the rest. "Use what you need."

"I can't take all this with me. What if something happens and we get separated? You'll need more than three hundred dollars."

"I have other ways of getting money. Take it. You may need it."

She hoped she wouldn't. She hoped she could get what she needed for a couple of hundred dollars and bring back the rest.

She hoped a lot of things. But hopes weren't the same thing as certainty. And if something happened to separate her from Brand while she was shopping for the recording supplies, she might need every penny she could get her hands on to find her way back to him.

The thought gave her a moment's pause. The idea that she wouldn't find her way back to him hadn't even entered her mind, she realized, even though logic told her it was a strong possibility. What if Brand was sending her off on this trip to the surveillance shop in order to give himself time to disappear?

She looked up to find him watching her with sharp blue eyes. "You're not going to ditch me as soon as I leave here, are you?"

He looked shocked by the suggestion. "I would never leave you to fend for yourself against Cortland."

"Maybe you think I'd just give it up when I got back here to find you gone. Is that what you think?"

He shook his head. "I know you'd go through with it anyway, if you thought it might prove my innocence."

He was right. She would.

"I don't leave my agents behind."

"I'm not one of your agents anymore."

"And I'm not an FBI special agent in charge anymore, either." He reached across the table and covered her hand. "I'll be here when you get back if it's at all within my power. I promise you."

She turned her hand palm up, twining her fingers with his. "Okay."

He rose from the table, tugging her to her feet. Pulling her close, he pressed a soft kiss against her temple. "You need to get a move on. Be careful. Take back roads—you memorized the map I gave you, right?"

She nodded. "I'll find the place. No worries."

He cradled her face between his big hands, bending to kiss her. It was a slow, hot kiss, full of barely leashed desire

and a darker, deeper emotion she was afraid to try to iden-
tify. "If anyone gives you any trouble, you get out of there,
okay? Get out of there and get yourself to a safe place. You
don't worry about me, promise?"

"I can't promise not to worry about you," she said, helpless to hide the feelings she knew must be shining in her eyes
as she gazed up at him.

He kissed her again. "Then promise to be safe."

"I promise to come back to you safely," she compromised.

With a sigh, he shook his head and walked her to the door.
"If you're not back here by four, I'm going to come looking
for you."

"I'll be back by four," she promised, and knew she'd move
heaven and earth to do so. There was no way she was going
to let Adam Brand leave her life one second before it was
necessary.

The drive to Tech Palace took only fifteen minutes, faster
than she'd anticipated, even with the brief stop she'd made
on the way. The place looked like a dilapidated warehouse
on the outside, with the words *Tech Palace* painted in peel-
ing, faded green on the weathered brick facade. But once
she entered the glass front door, she realized that the outside
was pure camouflage, designed to fool anyone who might
think the place was a prime target for burglary, robbery or
other mischief.

Inside, four men manned the well-appointed store. The
largest and oldest of the four stood at the front counter, dwarf-
ing the narrow space behind the shiny glass display cases.
He was built like a rhinoceros, and looked nearly as mean,
with a broad forehead and a square jaw that looked hewn
from granite. He was more than a head taller than Delilah,
who was not a particularly small woman, and his shoulder
span looked as if he were a football lineman in full pads. His

black T-shirt was tight enough to assure an observer that beneath his clothes, he was all hard muscle.

He looked up at her approach, his dark eyebrows converging over his misshapen nose. "Can I help you?"

She tried to look afraid, though she was more fascinated by the man than frightened. She'd bet he had one hell of a backstory, and her curious side wanted to hear all about it. "I need a small recording device that can't be easily spotted. I don't want to have to wear a wire or any kind of bulky receiver that someone could spot. Do you have something like that? With a remote receiver, maybe?"

"I can hook you up with that." Brand had said the people at Tech Palace weren't the curious types, but Delilah could see that the counter clerk was very curious. "You won't be recording a third-party conversation without consent, will you?"

"No. It'll be a conversation between me and my ex. He's been threatening me, but not in front of anyone else. He's an ex-cop, and so far the police seem to believe him more than me."

"Has he hurt you physically?" The clerk stopped in the middle of walking to one of the back shelves, turning to look at her with a fierce scowl. He looked as if he'd like to handle her problem himself.

"No," she said quickly. "It's not like that. But he's a cop, and he's threatened to frame me for stuff. Check kiting and fraud, stuff like that. He says he can plant the evidence and make me look like a hardened criminal. I don't know how to defend myself against that if he tries, but if I could record one of his threats, I might be able to preempt him."

The big man looked at her approvingly. "Smart girl. I've got just the thing you need." He reached up to the top shelf and pulled down a small box. "This is a watch with a powerful video recorder inside." He opened the box and displayed a normal-looking silver watch. "Just push this button and it starts recording. Also has four gigs of storage."

"What powers it?"

"There's a two-hour lithium battery inside. You can re-charge it by plugging it into your computer. That's how you download the audio and video as well. I can sell you a re-placement battery if you think you'll need it, but the installed battery should last through a lot of recharges."

She didn't want to take any chances of an equipment fail-ure. "I'll take the extra battery. I don't know how long it'll take to get him threatening me on the recording."

"Be prepared, I say." The man handed the watch to her. "Why don't we try it on, see if I need to adjust the band for you?"

She slipped the watch over her left wrist and snapped the clasp. It wasn't a snug fit, exactly, but it didn't slip around when she moved her arm. "Looks like it fits."

He showed her which of the buttons on the frame of the watch triggered the camera and microphone. "Just press that and everything starts recording. The camera is set up so that you should be able to fold your arms naturally with the watch arm in front and record everything without drawing any at-tention to yourself."

"Should I charge it when I get home?"

"Absolutely, but there's probably enough of a charge in it right now, if you run into that creep before you get home."

She managed a smile. "Good to know."

"You come back here if it doesn't work out. Maybe we can think up another way for you to get that jerk off your back."

"I appreciate the help."

He rang up her purchase, and when she handed over the cash, he didn't even raise an eyebrow. She had a feeling he saw a lot of cash transactions in his kind of business.

Outside, the day had warmed a bit, the sun cutting through

the winter chill. A digital sign on the bank down the street, where she'd parked her Camaro, showed that the temperature had risen above fifty degrees.

The sun on her face made her feel hopeful for the first time in days, giving her a little spring in her step as she crossed the road, heading for the bank parking lot. But she stopped short a half block away.

Someone was slowly circling her Camaro, studying it from all sides.

She started walking again before she drew attention to herself, trying to assess her options.

Then she remembered the watch still fastened around her wrist.

As casually as she could, she lifted her watch hand and pressed the record button the Tech Palace clerk had shown her. She made herself keep walking toward the bank, trying not to show any signs of interest in what was happening around her car. Slowly lifting her left hand to brush her hair back from her face, she took the opportunity to sneak one good look at the man as she passed the parking lot and kept going, her heart hammering in her chest.

He was tall and lean, dressed in jeans and a long-sleeved plaid flannel shirt over a black cotton T-shirt. His hair was a little long, curling down on the collar of the flannel shirt. It was as dark as a crow's wing, a good match to the olive skin tone of his neck. His eyes were hidden behind a pair of sunglasses, and a John Deere cap shaded the rest of his face, making it difficult to make out much about his features.

She stopped at the corner and took several deep breaths. What now? Was he just some redneck with a muscle-car fetish? Or was he connected to the people hunting Brand?

She slowly circled the bank building, reaching the parking lot from the other end. She stayed out of sight at the edge of the bank and sneaked a quick peek.

The man was gone.

The hair at the back of her neck prickled. She turned to look behind her, half expecting the man to be there. But there was no one.

She waited another minute or two, until the door of the bank swung open behind her, forcing her into movement so she wouldn't attract unwanted attention. She continued into the parking lot, keeping an eye out for the man in the John Deere cap.

But he'd disappeared completely.

She took the time to check around the frame of the Camaro, looking for signs of a tracker or anything the man might have placed on the vehicle while she wasn't looking. She even opened the hood and studied the engine for signs of tampering. She saw nothing.

So maybe he really had been nothing more than a car nut interested in the Camaro for its own sake, she decided as she settled behind the steering wheel and took several calming breaths. Still, she braced herself when she turned the key in the ignition, half-afraid she'd trigger a bomb.

But the only thing the ignition triggered was the smooth purr of the Camaro's 305-horsepower engine.

She didn't spot the man on her way out of Blakeville, but she still made a point of driving around for a while, taking side streets and circling back several times until she was reassured that she hadn't picked up any sort of tail. She finally headed back toward the cabin, forced to drive faster than she'd have liked in order to beat the deadline she and Brand had set.

It was five till four when she pulled up by the cabin. She hadn't even made it out of the Camaro when the cabin door opened and Brand strode out to meet her, gathering her into a bone-crushing embrace.

"Brand?" She wriggled to make him loosen his death grip on her.

His eyes blazed with a combination of relief and anger. "What the hell took so long? Four o'clock was the far outside range of our timeline."

"I'll explain everything if you'll stop squeezing all the air out of my lungs!" She managed to get her hands loose and reached up to cradle his worry-lined face. "I'm fine. Everything's okay. I just had a little scare, so I took some time to make sure I wasn't followed back here, that's all."

"Okay." He released a long breath. "Okay."

She rose to her tiptoes and lifted her face for a kiss. He complied, lightly at first, then with a burst of passion that left them both breathless.

"Let's go inside and you can tell me all about what happened."

She showed him the spy watch first. "This has a two-hour charge, which should be enough to record whatever happens at the meeting. It's both audio and video, which will be of extra value if Cortland himself meets with me." She carried her packages over to the table where the tablet computer lay charging and pulled off the watch. While she powered up the tablet, she pulled off the watch and removed the cover of the USB connector port. She plugged it into the tablet.

"Nice gadget," Brand murmured from just over her shoulder.

She patted the chair next to her. "Sit down and let's see if this nice gadget really works."

"You shot something already?" He settled onto the chair, pulling it closer to her. He smelled good. Woodsy, as if he'd spent part of his time outdoors while waiting for her to return.

"If I did this right, yes." Following the instructions included with the watch, she pressed Play on the media player and held her breath.

A remarkably clear image showed up on-screen. Ambient sounds—vehicle traffic, the sound of her own footsteps and her accelerated breathing—came through the speakers.

"There." She pointed at the tablet screen. The picture was a little wobbly, but she'd managed to capture the dark-haired man in the green John Deere cap. "I don't think there's a zoom function. If there is, I didn't use it."

Brand leaned closer. "He's really giving your car the once-over."

"I know. Gave me a scare, let me tell you."

Brand laid his hand on her back, between her shoulder blades, his touch unmistakably possessive. Delilah tried not to let his nearness distract her but found it impossible. Even through the layers of clothes between her body and his palm, the fiery heat of his touch spread liquid warmth through her body to settle in the center of her sex.

Would there ever be a time she wouldn't want him?

"I swear, I've seen that guy before," Brand murmured.

She looked up at him. "Where?"

"I don't know. I don't recognize him, exactly. But there's something about him that's familiar. I just don't know why."

"Do you think he could be connected to Cortland?"

"I don't think that's where I know him from." Brand nibbled his bottom lip, his brow furrowed. "In the FBI, we see so many faces passing through—suspects, victims, APBs, most-wanted lists—it could be any one of those."

"I didn't find any tampering. If you want, you can go take a look at the Camaro, see if I missed anything."

"I probably should," he said. "I doubt you'd have missed anything, though. You were always my most observant agent."

"Two sets of eyes are better than one," she said with a shrug, turning back to the tablet screen. She played back the video, concentrating on the man in the cap. There *was* something familiar about him, she realized, but for some reason she connected it to Cooper Security, not the FBI. Maybe she'd seen his face in some dossier for a case she'd worked, but like Brand, she couldn't place him.

Brand returned from outside. He shrugged off his leather jacket and laid it on the back of the sofa. "I didn't find anything, either."

She met him in the middle of the room, slipping her arms around his waist. He hugged her close. "What's this for?"

"Does it have to be for anything?" she asked, looking up into his curious blue eyes.

A smile carved lines in his face. "No. It doesn't." He lowered his mouth to hers, the kiss soft and undemanding.

The molten heat pooling low in her belly began to bubble. She slid her hands beneath his T-shirt, warming her fingers on his hot skin.

He jumped a little, laughing as he dragged his mouth from hers. "Cold fingers, Hammond!"

"They'll warm up soon enough." She lightly traced a path up his spine, lifting the shirt as she went.

He kissed her again, his mouth firm and demanding this time. She kissed him with answering heat, scraping her fingernails lightly across his shoulders until he groaned with pleasure.

He drew back long enough to shrug his T-shirt the rest of the way over his head. "I missed you while you were gone."

"Ditto." She pulled her sweater off and tossed it in the general direction of the sofa. Her jeans and panties followed in one slightly off-balance shimmy, and she reached behind herself to unhook her bra.

The room was chilly, making goose bumps rise across her flesh. Her nipples rose to taut peaks, and when Brand brushed the pad of his thumb across the left one, she gasped from the electric shock that ripped through her. Grinning,

Brand raised his other hand to her right breast and repeated the caress, making her suck in another breath.

"See?" he murmured, pressing a kiss to her collarbone. "We still have so much to learn about each other."

She grabbed the zipper of his jeans and tugged. "We'll see about that."

Chapter Fifteen

"You don't have to do this." Brand's heart felt like a lump of lead caught in his throat, throbbing with dread as he watched Delilah dress the next morning.

He'd always thought of himself first and foremost as an FBI agent, a man driven to protect the country he served no matter what the cost. It had been the only way he could do the job he'd taken on, sending men and women into danger. He'd respected that the people he led had their own reasons for wanting to protect their fellow citizens, and he'd been determined to never let his feelings get in the way of sending them out to do their jobs.

But watching Delilah gird herself for the battle she'd chosen had stripped him utterly of any objectivity he might have once had where she was concerned. She could die trying to prove his innocence. It was a sacrifice he wasn't willing to let her make.

She finished buttoning her blouse and turned to look at him. "I know I don't. But I'm going to."

"Don't do this for me."

"It's not just for you." She picked up the jeans she'd draped over a chair by the bed. "Cortland's had people killed. He's not going to stop if we stop. He's going to keep going after my brother and Rachel."

"It doesn't have to be you who stops him."

She pulled on her jeans and zipped them, then sat on the bed beside him. "I'm the one best positioned to do this. Think like the special agent in charge, not the lover."

She smelled good, fresh from the shower, making him wish he could pull her back into bed and keep her there. He cupped her jaw, sliding his thumb over her full bottom lip. "I don't think I can do that anymore."

"You have to." She pulled away from his touch and stood.

He tamped down his fear for her and tried to do as she asked. Think like an agent, not a man. "How do you plan to contact him?"

"I've already done it."

He arched his eyebrow. "When? How?"

"I stopped at a pay phone yesterday on my way to Blakeville to call the lumber mill."

Brand stared at her. "And you didn't think to tell me this?"

"I didn't want to worry you ahead of time."

"Did you actually talk to Cortland?"

"No, but I made an appointment with his secretary."

"Did you give her your real name?"

"No." Her lips curved slightly. "I figure the element of surprise will be in my favor."

"And you don't think that mystery man giving your Camaro the once-over has anything to do with your phone call?"

"I wasn't in Blakeville when I made the call, so how would Cortland know where I was going?"

"He wouldn't," Brand conceded. "What time is the meeting?"

"Eleven this morning."

A ripple of panic shot through him. "That's only a couple of hours."

"I know. That's why I'm dressing."

He scraped his hand over his beard. "I'd better get in the shower."

She put her hand out to stop him. "You can't go."

"Like hell I can't."

"Brand, if anyone sees you—"

"Nobody will see me."

"You can't know that."

"Damn it, Hammond!" He threw off the bedcovers and crossed to where she stood.

Her dark eyes dropped to take in his nakedness, then rose to meet his gaze, amusement gleaming in her expression. "You think you can distract me with your smokin'-hot body, Brand?"

He saw by the flush of pink beneath her golden skin that she wasn't exactly immune to his naked masculinity. "Maybe."

She flattened her hand on his chest to keep him from moving any closer. "Let me do this my way, Brand."

He wanted to argue, but the look in her eyes told him anything he said would be futile. "Okay. Do it your way."

She looked surprised and a little suspicious. "You gave in too easily."

He stepped back until he reached the bed, sitting and looking up at her. "I just know an unwinnable battle when I see one."

Her eyes remained narrowed, as if she was trying to ferret out the catch to his sudden acquiescence. "If I'm not back by four, get the hell out of here and don't worry about me."

"That's not possible."

"Fine. Get the hell out of here and worry about me to your heart's content." Her gaze fell to the bandage on his side. "You'll be okay to walk out of here, right?"

He nodded. "I'm nearly good as new."

She released a little sigh of frustration. "I'll do everything in my power to get back here by four. I promise."

He caught her hand and pulled her down to his lap. "You do that."

She slipped her arms around his neck, pressing her forehead to his. "If I get this right, your whole ordeal could be over today."

He didn't know whether he wanted to believe her or not. He'd thought there was nothing in the world he wanted more than to clear his name and return to his job at the FBI. But going back to Washington meant leaving Delilah behind. Ripping her out of his life yet again, maybe forever this time.

"That's what you want, isn't it?" she asked.

He looked up at her, deep into her dark eyes, and tried to read her own emotions there. But all he saw were his own questions reflected back at him.

"Yes," he answered, and tried to mean it. "But I don't want you to go out there unprotected."

"I can protect myself."

He shook his head. "At least give me some way to track you."

She arched her eyebrows. "What do you have in mind?"

"There's a miniature GPS tracker in the stashed bag we picked up. I put it there in case I had trouble finding where I'd buried it." He nodded toward the bag. "It should still have plenty of battery power to work."

"What if they frisk me?"

"Put it in your bra."

She laughed softly. "You sound like Megan Pike—Jesse's sister," she elaborated at his look of confusion. "She's a big proponent of female operatives hiding things in their bras. She says most men are hesitant to search your bra, and if they do, you have worse problems than being caught carrying a hidden object."

"Wise woman. The tracker's small enough that you should easily be able to conceal it."

She rose from his lap and bent to kiss him lightly. "Okay. But let's hurry and get it set up. I want to scope the place out a little before I walk into the lion's den."

He retrieved the small tracker, which was a little bigger than a flash drive, and handed it to Delilah. She tucked it under her left breast and held out her arms. "Do you see it?"

He studied her breasts, trying to be clinical about it. "No." He grabbed his phone from the bedside table and called up the tracking device. The coordinates of her location came through and he checked them against his map application. Right on the money.

"Okay, then. I'd better go." She kissed him again. "Don't come after me if I don't come back. Call Jesse Cooper and give him the GPS coordinates. Let him find me. You get out of here while you can."

No way in hell was he going to agree to that, but he didn't tell her so. Instead, he forced himself to watch her go, his heart in his throat. He remained still even though his muscles bunched with the need for action, waiting until he heard the door close behind her and the Camaro engine roar to life before he moved.

She'd been right to be suspicious of his easy acquiescence, he thought with a smile as he showered quickly and dressed for travel. Because there was something he knew about the cabin property that she didn't: there was a shed just out of view from the cabin where Liz Vaughn had kept a four-wheel-drive truck.

If he was lucky, there was still gas in the tank from the last time she'd visited. Even if he was unlucky, he and Delilah had bought several gallons of gas for the generator. He could scavenge enough fuel from their stash to get him to the service station up the road.

Either way, he was going to make damned sure Delilah had backup for her meeting with Wayne Cortland.

TRAVISVILLE WAS A small town, not much bigger than Delilah's hometown of Bitterwood, and Cortland Lumber was by far the largest company in town, at least in terms of square footage. It sprawled across several acres and contained not only the sawmill itself but a retail property, a shipping area and several hundred acres of trees from which Cortland harvested the lumber he sold under the Cortland label.

The place was bustling even that late in the morning, full of contractors and individual customers alike, moving at quick, workmanlike paces through the floor-to-ceiling displays of building supplies the lumber mill sold.

She wasn't the only woman in the place, so she didn't draw much extra attention, to her relief. She was able to reach the part of the retail store where the woman who'd answered her call had told her she'd find the company offices. Lining the wall behind the front counter were several closed doors, all marked with names and titles. The one directly behind the counter had a narrow gold plaque with *Wayne Cortland, President* engraved in bold, straight letters.

The front-desk clerk was a heavyset man with dark gray eyes and a florid complexion. He pasted on a smile at her approach. "How can I help you today, ma'am?"

"I have an appointment with Mr. Cortland at eleven a.m."

The man's sandy eyebrows rose slightly. "I'll tell his assistant you're here." He picked up a phone, pushed a button and spoke to someone on the other end. He hung up the phone and nodded. "Mr. Cortland wants you to wait in the sawmill office. It's just out that door to the right. Can't miss it." He pointed toward the side exit.

"Thank you." Delilah kept her pace unhurried, determined not to appear nervous or overly eager. She'd told Cortland's assistant she was interested in contracting with Cortland for supplies for rental cabins on some land she owned in the mountains. She'd hoped—she still hoped—that such a financial inducement might convince Cortland to meet with her himself.

She wasn't sure what she'd expected from the sawmill office, but the room she stepped into wasn't it. It was barely a shed, full of dusty equipment under dustier plastic covers. In one corner, a tall wooden box a little larger than a storage chest took up a large portion of the area.

The only light in the room went away when the door closed behind her.

"Hello?" she called into the gloom. But she could see herself that nobody else was there.

Alarm creeping up her neck, she turned back to the door and turned the knob. It rattled uselessly in her hand.

She banged on the door. "Hello?"

Though she heard shuffling footsteps outside the shed, nobody answered her calls. She tried the doorknob again, in case it was just stuck, but it didn't budge. It was locked, and apparently from the outside.

Faint light trickled through the narrow space beneath the door, easing some of the darkness inside the windowless shed. Delilah pulled her keys from her pocket and engaged the penlight attached to the chain, letting the narrow beam of light play around the small shed. She saw nothing she hadn't seen before. Nothing that would convince her this was all a mistake that would soon be rectified.

She was in trouble. No pretending otherwise—this clearly wasn't any sort of office, and someone had followed her out here and locked her in. She had to assume they had a pretty good idea who she was and, most likely, why she was there.

She had to find a way out of here, and fast.

There were no windows and only the one door, unless a second exit was hidden behind the pieces of equipment blocking her view of half the room. She picked her way through them, hoping to find another outlet near the back of the shed, but just as she'd squeezed her way between a large table saw and a battered-looking copy machine, she heard the door behind her open.

She whirled around in time to see something fly into the room and explode with a bang. A fine mist began to spray into the shed. At the first burning whiff of the gas, she realized what it was.

A tear-gas canister.

One of the most beneficial parts of working for Cooper Security had been the training program that Jesse Cooper had required of all employees, agents and support staff alike. Field agents had undergone extra training, of course, including riot-control training—from both sides of the tear gas.

"Think like a rioter," Jesse had warned them during the training sessions. "There may come a time when you're on the other end of the tear gas, and you have to know how to function."

They'd gone through dozens of scenarios, dealt with the painful effects of the pepper gas, and over time they'd internalized the procedures to limit the effects of tear-gas exposure.

Prophylaxis was, of course, the most obvious answer. Suiting up and wearing a mask wasn't an option in the tiny shed, but one of the dust sheets over the old equipment could block most of the gas if she could get herself under it.

Trying to keep her head turned away from the gas, Delilah held her breath and tugged at the sheet on the copier. It snagged on one side of the machine but pulled free, and she covered her face and torso with the plastic, edging to the far side of the shed to keep the worst of the gas from reaching her.

But the shed was tiny, and she didn't dare close herself up completely in the plastic sheeting or she'd suffocate. It didn't take long for some of the pepper gas to reach her nose and face, making her eyes and nose leak and her chest constrict with pain.

She heard the door open again, and two people entered the shed. Through the plastic sheeting, she made out only tall, broad silhouettes with misshapen heads. It took her a second to realize they were wearing gas masks to block out the tear gas.

They surrounded her, grabbing her arms and legs through the plastic sheeting. She kicked out at them, but the plastic limited her motion too much for her to be very effective, and as the sheeting came loose, more of the tear gas poured under it, exacerbating her pain and rendering her nearly blind from the effects of the pepper in her eyes.

They picked her up and carried her only a few feet before depositing her inside something. A door closed, shutting out the light and the pepper gas. A moment later, the world turned on its head and she slammed against the hard back of the container into which her captors had shoved her.

She felt her makeshift prison swaying. They were moving her, entombed in this coffinlike box.

She tried to shout, but the effects of the pepper gas had turned her voice into little more than a gasping croak. She struggled with the plastic sheeting, feeling the first smothering panic of diminishing oxygen, made worse by her gas-irritated lungs. She finally got her face free of the plastic and took a couple of rasping breaths, willing herself to ignore the burning pain on her skin and in her streaming eyes.

She tried shouting again, but it was too late. She felt a hard thud as the box she was in hit a solid surface and slid with a scrape against what sounded like a metal floor. There was a loud, rattling clang of a door being shut, and what little daylight had crept through the seams of the box disappeared, plunging her into claustrophobic darkness.

An engine roared to life, somewhere very nearby. Then

she felt movement again, more subtle and indirect. She must be in the back of a truck, she realized. They were moving her.

But to where?

Chapter Sixteen

The GPS was still tracking, Brand reassured himself with a quick look at the app, which meant that they hadn't found the device she had tucked in her bra. But that was the end of the good news.

Brand had seen it all go down, powerless to make a move. Perched on a hill a quarter mile away, he'd trained his binoculars on the lumber mill, spotting Delilah's Camaro as it entered the parking area.

He'd watched her head into the lumber-mill showroom, and, moments later, leave by a side door and enter an adjacent shed, her exit so quick and unobtrusive that he might have missed it if he hadn't seen two men slide into position behind her with the secretive stealth of soldiers. The second she was inside the shed, they'd closed the door and locked it behind her, then taken up positions on either side of the door.

Moments later, another man had arrived, handing one of the two guards a canvas bag. After donning a gas mask and handing another to the other guard, the man on the right had pulled something small and cylindrical from the bag, unlocked the door and thrown the cylinder inside before shutting the door again.

Tear-gas canister, Brand thought, desperately trying to come up with a way to help her without getting into an unwinnable gunfight with the two goons guarding the shack.

The thought of Delilah forced to deal with tear gas inside that shed made his blood boil, but he had to keep his head. She'd survive a tear-gas attack. It would hurt like hell for a while, but she'd survive. If he ran down there, guns blazing, she'd be a sitting duck.

The two men in the masks went into the shed a few minutes later and emerged, finally, carrying a large wooden box about the size of a coffin.

Brand had no doubt Delilah was inside the box, and the GPS tracker proved him right a few minutes later, as he followed its frequent updates of her position on his burner phone.

The men had loaded the box into a white panel truck with no logos or other markings on its sides. They had a decent head start, since Brand had to trek through the woods to get back to Liz's truck. He'd made decent time on the highway, using the GPS tracker's coordinates to guide him toward the panel truck's destination.

The tracker finally stopped moving. Had they stopped somewhere for good? Even though the roads in this part of the county were notorious speed traps, he gunned the truck's engine, risking the attention of police. Hell, it would probably be better in the long run if he picked up a few blue lights for the ride. He had a feeling he could use all the backup he could muster.

He never should have agreed to let her meet Cortland alone. He'd clearly been expecting her.

But how? Had someone spotted her in Blakeville and reported back to Cortland? Maybe that dark-haired man in the John Deere cap who'd been scoping out her Camaro at the bank parking lot?

The next update from the tracker showed she was still in the same place. They'd definitely reached the end of the line.

But where was that? The GPS map showed she was located

on Bachelor Road, a two-lane that wound through woods and past the occasional storage warehouse or two on the edge of Travisville. Maybe Cortland owned land in the area. A warehouse?

He ended up passing the place before he spotted the panel truck parked around the side of a nondescript, one-story cinder-block building in the middle of nowhere. There were no signs on the building, nothing that might signify it was in use. But the panel truck sat there, the back doors open. Brand watched in the rearview mirror as two men emerged from the building, locked the door behind them and crouched beside the building.

A sharp curve in the road forced Brand to pay attention to his driving, and by the time he checked the rearview mirror again, the building was no longer in sight.

THEY'D STOPPED SOMEWHERE, and her captors had taken the box from the truck and deposited it in a very quiet place. She heard the sound of footsteps moving away from her at a rapid pace, dying away to nothing after a door creaked and clicked closed.

She waited a moment, listening for more sound. She heard nothing in particular, but the prickle of hair on the back of her neck told her that, wherever they'd deposited her and her makeshift cage, she wasn't alone.

"Hello?" she called, her voice still raspy.

There was no answer.

Maybe she'd been wrong. Maybe she was all alone here after all. She turned her attention away from what might lie outside the box and tried to focus on how to escape the inside of the box.

But even with slivers of light seeping into the box through the seams, she could barely see. The plastic sheeting had stopped a lot of the tear gas, but she hadn't emerged un-scathed. Tears still streamed from her eyes and mucus trickled from her nose and down her throat, forcing her to cough and sneeze and generally make a sorry mess of her clothes.

But she knew her body's reaction to the pepper gas was also its best means of getting rid of the offending chemicals, so she didn't worry too much about what she'd look like when she finally found a way out of the box.

She gave up trying to see and focused on feeling her way around the confines of the box, looking for a weak board or a loose nail. But a rattle right outside the box froze her in place.

She followed the sound. It was coming from the right corner of the box directly behind her.

She turned her head to face the noise, squinting with pain when the box opened suddenly, letting bright daylight pour into her formerly dark prison.

A dark, man-shaped silhouette blocked part of the light, and for a moment, her heart beat a little faster with the certainty that Brand had ignored her warning and come after her.

But as her streaming eyes adjusted to the brightness, she saw that the man standing in front of her was shorter and more slightly built than Brand. His face bore the first telltale lines of impending middle age, putting him somewhere in his mid-to-late thirties. His hair was sandy and a little on the wavy side, falling almost to his shoulders in a blunt, shapeless cut. His eyes were clear green and watchful as he stepped back from the box and waited.

She blinked back the tears filling her eyes and tried to focus on his face. There was something familiar about him. It took a second to place him, but when she did, she felt a ripple of relief.

"Cav."

Nolan Cavanaugh's mouth curved slightly. "Who?" But the look in his eyes didn't match his words. She saw a warning there. "Never mind. You just do what I tell you and everything will be okay."

He must think the place was bugged. Hell, he was probably right. And if he was undercover, she didn't want to be the one to expose him to Wayne Cortland. "What do you want me to do?"

"Sit there at the table. I have some questions to ask you."

She walked over to the table and chairs he indicated. Other than the box, they were the only things in the room, save for a few heavy-looking pieces of equipment that lined the walls on almost every side. She looked at the equipment, frowning. What a strange way to set up a warehouse.

She sat in one of the two chairs. Cavanaugh took the other, looking meaningfully at her until she focused on him again. "Mr. Cortland would like to know why you contacted him."

"I wanted to make a deal." All her internal alarms were clanging like crazy. If Cortland had cared what she wanted, why hadn't he simply met with her? Why gas her and spirit her away from the lumber mill?

Something about the layout of this warehouse bothered her. What was the point of lining the walls with heavy equipment?

"What's in those boxes?" she asked Cavanaugh, nodding toward the rows of machines, where cardboard boxes covered nearly every available surface.

"I'm here to ask questions, not answer them," Cavanaugh said patiently, though she saw his gaze shift around the room as if he hadn't thought to check his surroundings before now.

Something was wrong here. Very wrong. She looked Cavanaugh over quickly, forced to make a decision. He was either on her side or on Cortland's. Which was it?

He wasn't armed. And even if he was on Cortland's payroll for real, he had to be low on the totem pole. So why would they have sent him to interrogate her?

"Why you?" she asked.

His green eyes met hers, and he saw what she was asking.

"A test of loyalty, I suppose." His tone was flat, but his eyes were sending out messages about his true intent.

He was on her side.

She got up out of the chair, confident he wouldn't do anything to stop her. "This setup is all wrong."

"Please come back and sit down," he said, resignation in his voice.

She crossed to the nearest door and tried it. Locked, from the outside.

She moved from the door to the nearest machine, a table saw. She rested her hand on it for support to reach for the cardboard box that lay near the saw, but the whole machine moved, drawing her gaze to the floor. Caster wheels had been attached to the legs of the table. To all of the pieces of machinery, she saw with a quick scan of the room.

The klaxons in her head growing more urgent, she opened the top of the cardboard box and looked inside. The box was half-filled with nails, screws and other small metal objects. A quick look in the next three boxes revealed the same thing.

Shrapnel, she thought, her heart in her throat.

"Delilah, come sit down and let's get on with this," Cavanaugh called, sounding frustrated.

She hurried across the room to the only other door she saw. It was locked as well, but she heard movement outside. The unmistakable sound of tape being pulled from a spool. There was a soft thud that rattled the door and a couple of patting noises against the wood.

Delilah backed away from the door, her heart in her throat. "It's a bomb."

Cavanaugh rose from his chair, knocking it backward. "A bomb?"

She turned to look at him. "All the machinery is set on casters—any movement will send them flying with nothing to slow them down. The boxes are full of nails, screws and other shrapnel. And I just heard what I'm pretty sure was someone attaching a block of C-4 or some other explosive to the door. They're rigging this place to blow, and they've made damned sure that anyone inside will be flayed or crushed or both."

Cavanaugh's eyes widened with fear. "I knew I shouldn't have taken this damned job."

"Who put you onto it?" She moved close to him, keeping her voice low, in case his fears about the place being bugged were right.

"I can't tell you that," he whispered back.

"Okay. Who told you to come here to interrogate me? Was it Cortland himself?"

"No. It was another guy. He never gave his name."

"What did he look like?"

"Dark hair, clean-cut, blue eyes."

"Tall? Short? Thin?"

"My height. A little burly."

Cavanaugh's description sent a little shiver up her spine. "How old?"

Cavanaugh's gaze had begun to wander around the room, wide with growing terror. "How long before they blow this place?"

"I don't know. How old was the man who sent you here?"

"I don't know—late fifties? Maybe early sixties."

"Son of a bitch." Well, that answered at least one question that had been nagging her since she came back to Bitterwood to follow up on Sutton Calhoun's investigation into the Bitterwood murders. She'd believed all along that whoever had been behind the murders had an ally in the local police force.

Now she knew who the ally was. "We have to get out of here."

"They'll kill us if we try."

"They're going to kill us anyway," she growled, her gaze

wandering across the small building. There wasn't much room to maneuver, even if she could use the machines to rig some sort of shelter. She discarded that idea quickly—depending on the kind of explosive, crouching behind a heavy piece of equipment with big, sharp blades was a damned good way to sign your own death warrant.

They needed to get out of the warehouse. Now.

Her gaze snagged on the only bit of decoration in the small building—a dun-colored area rug that sat by itself in the middle of the floor. Why was there a rug in a warehouse?

Working a desperate hunch, Delilah ran to the rug and gave it a sharp pull. It slid aside, revealing a square of concrete that looked different from the rest of the floor.

"Cav, come help me with this." There was no handle, but a small depression in one side of the block created a fingerhold. She tugged at it, straining against the heavy slab of concrete.

"Wait!" Cavanaugh ran across the room and grabbed something off one of the machines. It was a metal rod, she saw as he slipped one end under the narrow opening she'd managed to create. The rod levered the slab up enough for them to push it out of the way, revealing a metal ladder extending down into a dark basement.

"After you," Delilah said, nodding toward the opening.

Cavanaugh didn't need to be coaxed. He scrambled down ahead of her, leaving her to follow. She landed next to Cavanaugh in the small square of light pouring through the trapdoor from the warehouse above.

Delilah patted the pocket of her jeans and found, to her surprise, that she still had her keys. She pulled out the keychain and tried the penlight. It cast a thin beam across their new surroundings, revealing a long, narrow basement. The walls and floor were hard-packed dirt, held in place by wooden beams. Not as sturdy a structure as she'd hoped, she thought with sinking heart.

"This place can't survive a blast." Cavanaugh grimaced.

"No, it can't." She tried to keep her wits, but it was hard concentrating on their surroundings when she had a ticking clock in her head. How long before the whole place blew to kingdom come? Minutes? Seconds?

The cellar was dank and musty but gave no real sense of disuse. She spotted a few cobwebs in the corners, but the dirt floor was clear of clutter, and the penlight showed fresh footprints in the dirt floor near the back of the small room where there was a dark recess, as if an alcove had been dug into the wall.

She crossed to the alcove and directed the beam of her penlight into the darkness. The beam bounced off a flat metal surface.

"That's a door," Cavanaugh said.

It was, indeed, a door. A steel-reinforced door similar to the one she'd had on the rental house she'd lived in back in Maybridge, Alabama. She'd added the steel door on Jesse's suggestion, since some of the jobs Cooper Security worked invited retaliation from people who'd find a normal wooden door no obstacle.

There was no dead bolt on the door, just a knob lock. On this side there wasn't even a keyhole, only a thin-edged button that turned easily at Delilah's touch. She turned the knob and pushed the steel door outward.

Beyond the door was only darkness.

She flashed her penlight across the opening. The beam bounced off the walls of a narrow tunnel. The floor was hard-packed dirt, but as far as the flashlight beam would go, she saw only concrete walls.

"What the hell is this?" Cavanaugh asked, gazing into the tunnel with narrowed eyes.

Delilah took a step into the tunnel. "Hopefully, a way out."

THE ROAD WOUND on for a mile, it seemed, before Brand could find a place to turn around. He had even tried a U-turn a couple of times, but oncoming traffic had thwarted him each time, forcing him to continue forward until he could find a better place.

By the dashboard clock, almost five minutes had passed since he'd driven by the warehouse. Five excruciating minutes filled with an endless stream of nightmare images. Brand had been in the FBI for more than twenty years. In that time, he'd seen a wide range of the evils men did to each other, the lengths to which the truly depraved could go.

And still, he had to take care on this second approach, with the clock ticking time away, because he couldn't be sure just how many people were guarding the storage building in the middle of nowhere.

But when the cinder-block building came back into view, there was no one around, and the panel truck was gone.

He pulled off the road and parked in an empty gravel lot about thirty yards from the building. He grabbed his binoculars from the seat beside him and lifted them to his eyes for a better look.

At first, the building seemed ordinary. An older building, grimy on the outside and probably equally dirty on the inside. There were only a few windows in the place, set high on the walls, and they were too thick with dust to see inside.

He could make out the shape of a door near the end of the building on the side he faced. As he directed the binoculars toward that door, a thin wire caught his attention. It seemed to be strung up all the way around the building, held in place at intervals by strips of duct tape the same pale color as the concrete cinder blocks of the building. Every four or five feet, a square block of what looked like putty had been pressed against the building.

Brand's heart skipped a couple of beats as he realized what he was seeing.

C-4 plastic explosive.

Detonators stuck out from the explosive, rigged to the wire, which was probably attached to a timer somewhere on the building's exterior.

He was out of the car before he could stop and think, driven only by a primal urge to get inside that building and get Delilah out before it blew. He had no doubt she was still inside. Why bring her out here and then rig the building if the intention wasn't to blow her up inside?

A passing pickup truck honked as he darted out in front of it, but he didn't care, picking up speed as he reached the other side of the road. From there, he was faced with an almost ninety-degree incline about six feet up to the flattened clearing where the cinder-block building stood.

He reached for a handhold in the dry grass of the slope, grimacing against the answering pain in his injured side. His hand slipped and he stumbled into the hillside, hitting awkwardly on his shoulder. A burst of pain from the point of impact was swallowed immediately by a bone-jarring boom. His ears began to ring as the sky opened above him, raining down debris on top of where he crouched.

He pressed himself flat, covering his head to protect himself from the onslaught, his brain swirling with a toxic cocktail of fear and denial. That couldn't have been the building exploding. It wasn't possible. He could still reach the building before time ran out.

That was how it had to be. Anything else was unthinkable.

On the road behind him, vehicles hit the brakes with a squeal. The shower of debris had stopped enough for Brand to spare a glance at the road. Chunks of cinder blocks and twisted pieces of metal littered the blacktop, making it next to impossible for traffic to pass. Cars and trucks had begun to pile up on either side of the debris field, and some of the drivers had gotten out of their vehicles to stare.

Dread squeezing his chest like a vise, Brand backed away from the incline so he could see what lay beyond the rise. It took a long, surreal moment to process what he saw.

The cinder-block building had been sheared in two. The bottom blocks remained, like jagged broken teeth, but the top six feet of the building had exploded into dust and debris. Mangled steel and wood machines sprawled across the now open area like battle dead, torn beyond any hope of salvation. Lifting the binoculars slowly to his eyes, he saw that nails and screws had embedded themselves in the pieces of shattered wood, shot there by the force of the explosion.

No one inside that building could have survived.

"Hey, mister. Are you okay?" The voice seemed muffled and far away. Brand looked up and saw a bearded man in a camouflage jacket looking at him through dark, wary eyes. The man waved his hand toward Brand's shirt. "You're bleeding."

Brand looked down at his shoulder and saw the head of a nail sticking out of his arm. "I guess I took some shrapnel," he said. His voice sounded as if he were speaking from the inside of a jar.

The faint sound of sirens bled through the cottony cocoon of deafness. The police, probably. Definitely fire and emergency medical technicians.

If Delilah was here, she'd tell him to get his butt in gear and get out of here before the cops showed up.

But Delilah wasn't here.

Not anymore.

He slumped to the ground, resting his back against the hillside, and waited for the police to arrive.

Chapter Seventeen

The tunnel shook violently for a long moment. Delilah lost her footing, crashing into the cold concrete wall with a painful thud. Behind her, Cavanaugh uttered a low, feral growl of profanities.

Delilah pushed herself upright again, wincing as the tremors continued for a few seconds. "There went the explosives."

"Think it's going to cave in on us?"

There were alarming sounds behind them in the tunnel, and she had a feeling the basement had collapsed from the force of the explosion. But they were far enough in the tunnel now that they should be safe.

At least, she hoped so.

"I think we're good." She sounded more confident than she felt.

"Where do you think this goes?"

"If I had to guess, this might have been an old moonshiner route at one time. Cortland probably knows about all the nooks and crannies of these hills, especially as pertains to criminal enterprises."

"Just be careful. We could come out in the middle of some militia enclave," Cavanaugh warned as they started forward.

She'd thought of that possibility. But there was no going back.

The tunnel branched into two passageways about a hundred yards farther along. Delilah stopped at the fork and checked her watch. Already one-thirty. Two and a half hours to get back to Brand before he continued on the run without her.

"Which way?" Cavanaugh asked.

"Any idea which direction they go? North, south, east, west?"

Cavanaugh thought for a moment. "The left one goes southeast. The one on the right heads straight south."

"Are we north or south of Travisville?"

"Just north."

"So one of these tunnels could, feasibly, take us right back to the lumber mill?"

Cavanaugh looked at her, his mouth open. "You're not suggesting—"

"Which way?"

Cavanaugh's eyes narrowed. "Southeast."

"Then we're going south." Delilah headed down the right tunnel.

"Damn it! This is the one that probably goes to the lumber mill."

Delilah turned around to face Cavanaugh. "I know."

"Why the hell are you going back there?"

"Because they won't be expecting me." She nodded toward the other passageway. "If you want to go that way, feel free."

Cavanaugh's eyes narrowed. "I'm just a computer guy. I've never wanted to be in the middle of all this cloak-and-dagger mess."

Delilah felt a sliver of sympathy for him. This cloak-and-dagger mess, as he'd called it, wasn't something most people could deal with. She'd chosen it because she couldn't imagine anything this kind of life could throw at her would be any worse than what she'd already lived through, but from what she knew of Nolan Cavanaugh, he'd had a pretty good life growing up. His father was wealthy, his parents still happily married, his family intact.

He'd gotten sucked into this whole mess because he'd uncovered information that brought down a lot of very powerful people. His life was in danger because he'd done the right thing once and earned a target on his back.

"Go," she said. "Get out of here. Is there anyone you can trust?"

"Evie Cooper," he said quietly.

"Then contact her as soon as you can. The Coopers will take care of you."

"I know." Cavanaugh frowned. "I have information about Cortland. What if I don't make it out alive?"

Delilah looked at her watch again. "Can you tell me what you know?"

"It won't be admissible. Hearsay."

She tapped her watch. "There's a camera in this watch." She pointed the penlight at Cavanaugh's face, making him squint. Positioning the watch, she pressed the record button. "Tell me what you know."

BRAND WAVED OFF the paramedics who showed up looking for victims. The nail in his arm hadn't gone in very deeply; he'd plucked it out with little pain or drama. His tetanus shots were up-to-date, so he should be okay if he cleaned it up soon. Meanwhile, he had changed his mind, deciding to steer clear of the police who had converged on the place in droves.

It was what Delilah would have wanted him to do.

There was no way to drive away; the emergency vehicles had blocked both lanes of the access road. Traffic was backed up for miles now. Brand settled down in the cab of Liz's truck and waited for someone to tell the police about his attempted dash toward the scene of the crime.

And, if he was brutally honest with himself, he was also

waiting for the paramedics to wheel out a body bag from the ruins of the warehouse.

But an hour passed with neither of those things happening. The police seemed more interested in picking through the crime scene, gathering the bits and pieces of wire and detonators amid the mangled ruins of the building. The paramedics waited patiently to the side for the whole hour before the jeans-clad detective who seemed to be in charge came out of the building and shook his head at them. The paramedics packed up their things and drove away, clearing a path for traffic to start moving again.

Brand sat like a stone, gazing at the ruins of the building with his heart in his throat. Why had the detective sent the paramedics away? Wouldn't they be the ones to carry a body out?

Maybe the detective had called for the coroner.

But another thirty minutes passed without any sign of a medical examiner's wagon, and even some of the police started to disperse, allowing more room for the backed-up traffic to pass through.

Brand didn't want to leave, not without knowing what had happened to Delilah. But lingering here much longer would only put him directly in the crosshairs of the local cops, a complication he definitely didn't need.

Think, Brand. Why do you think she was in the building?

Because of the GPS tracker.

He pulled out his phone and checked the tracker program. But the tracker light didn't show up at all.

He laid his head back against the headrest, his heart aching. She must have been in the building.

Unless someone had found the tracker, he realized. What if they'd sent the tracker off in that box to lead him on a wild-goose chase?

A dangerous flood of hope shot through him as he realized

he'd seen them lock her inside the shed. Seen them throw the gas in. But he'd never seen them put her in the box.

What if she'd never been in the box?

He had to go back to the lumber mill and get a look inside that shed.

SHE'D LET CAVANAUGH have the penlight from her keychain. She hoped the battery would last long enough to get him safely out of the tunnel, because navigating in the dark was a pain in the backside. The air was chilly but stale, though there was clearly some sort of ventilation system at work, because she didn't feel any effects of limited oxygen. And unless her imagination was playing tricks on her, she thought she could see the faintest hint of light a hundred yards ahead.

She could make out the concrete walls of the tunnel, the wooden supports that crisscrossed the structure to keep it from caving in. It wasn't the most professional job of tunnel building she'd ever seen, but someone had gone to a hell of a lot of trouble to make sure the passageway didn't collapse.

It was big enough to accommodate the smuggling of almost anything, she thought. Drugs, guns, explosives, even people. So why had Cortland blown up the building? Was it purely to kill her and Cavanaugh? Or had they been planning to destroy the warehouse all along, and using the explosion to get rid of her and Cavanaugh was just a stroke of luck?

The air was cooler and fresher as she neared the lighter part of the tunnel. The wall took a sudden, sharp turn, revealing an opening ahead. The light was painfully bright to her still-sensitive eyes, sending a jolt of fiery pain shooting through her head and a fresh flood of tears streaming from her eyes. She blinked the tears away, standing still until her eyes adjusted enough to make out metal bars at the open end of the tunnel.

With a grimace, she moved carefully toward the metal

grille, staying close to the wall to minimize her visibility to anyone who might be on the outside. Cold air poured through the opening, scattering chill bumps over her skin as she edged her way to the metal bars.

It took a moment to realize she was gazing down on the back side of Cortland Lumber.

BRAND HADN'T TAKEN two steps inside the gates of Cortland Lumber when a man in a dark green baseball cap seemed to glide out of the shadows to stand in front of him. The man was tall, nearly Brand's height, but lean and wiry, as if he'd missed a few meals over the last little while. He was backlit by the early afternoon sun, but Brand could make out enough of his dark features to realize he was looking at the man Delilah had filmed outside the bank in Blakeville.

Once again, Brand felt a glimmer of recognition. He knew this man, somehow. Had seen his face before.

"Don't be stupid," the man said.

"Who the hell are you?" Brand asked.

The man smiled grimly, and Brand felt a click in his brain. That smile, feral and roguish, had been on the wall of every post office in America at one time. It had also been posted on the bulletin board in Brand's own office until just a few short years ago, when the man in question had died in an explosion in the South American republic of Sanselmo.

"You're dead," Brand said.

"Do I really have to quote Mark Twain?" the man asked.

"You blew up in a munitions-factory explosion in Tesoro almost four years ago. The FBI confirmed your identity through DNA."

"DNA can be faked." Sinclair Solano, formerly one of the FBI's most wanted for acts of terror against U.S. interests in South America, gave such a nonchalant shrug that Brand blinked a couple of times to make sure he hadn't been knocked cold by the warehouse explosion and was just dreaming this bizarre encounter.

"What do you want?" he asked when Solano didn't disappear.

"To stop you from getting yourself killed."

Brand shook his head, still not sure he wasn't hallucinating. "You do realize I'm an FBI agent."

"Not at the moment," Solano reminded him.

"You were in Blakeville yesterday. Outside the bank."

Solano's eyes narrowed but he didn't respond.

"What are you up to?"

"Someone sent me to keep an eye on you and Delilah Hammond."

"Who?"

Solano's eyebrows lifted, but he didn't answer.

"Get out of my way."

Solano's gaze scanned the lumberyard before turning back to Brand. "I know about the explosion. I know Delilah was in the building. I'm sorry."

Brand's heart skipped a beat. "How can you know?"

"I planted a bug in the air-vent system in the lumberyard office," Solano said. "I've been monitoring conversations the last few days. They delivered Delilah and a man named Dixon to the Bradley Road warehouse and blew it up with them inside. It's all recorded. You'll have the evidence you need. But you have to get out of here before you mess up everything."

Brand shook his head. "Why would you do such a thing?"

"Because, believe it or not, I'm not one of the bad guys." His face darkened with old regret. "Not anymore."

A customer passed them on the way inside the lumberyard. He gave them a curious look as he walked by. Brand followed the man's gaze and saw that the bloody patch on the shoulder of his jacket had begun to spread.

"Delilah's not dead," Brand said, needing to believe it.

Solano's answering look was full of pity. "You have to get out of here now, before Cortland's men spot you."

A couple of men came out of the office even as Solano was speaking, their gazes sweeping over the lumberyard. Brand walked slowly sideways, toward the exit, taking care not to look as if he were in a hurry. "I need to speak to you again."

"I'll be in touch."

Brand paused, gazing warily at the man he'd spent years loathing for his crimes. "How do I know I can trust you?"

Solano gave him a long, hard look. "You don't." He turned and disappeared through a narrow path between stacks of lumber.

Brand had parked up the hill and entered the lumberyard on foot, thinking he'd be less conspicuous that way. But he wondered if he'd been thinking at all. Everything he'd done since the warehouse blast had been fueled by emotion—grief, rage, hope, desperation—instead of rational thought. He'd entered the lumberyard with no plan, no protection, dripping blood and looking like a shell-shocked battle survivor.

He had to get himself under control. If Delilah *was* alive, she didn't need him falling apart and screwing up everything they'd tried to accomplish.

Reaching the truck on wobbly legs, he pulled himself into the cab and sat in the quiet for a moment, trying to forget everything he was feeling. He needed to tuck those emotions out of the way, save them for later, when he had time and space to stop thinking and start feeling again.

Solano had said Cortland and his men believed Delilah and someone named Dixon had expired in the explosion, which meant she'd definitely been in the warehouse. But the police detective had clearly indicated to the paramedics that they'd found no one inside the building after what had seemed like a pretty thorough search.

So if Delilah had been in the building, but wasn't there when it exploded, where had she gone? Brand had seen the men taking the box into the warehouse, but his eyes had been off the place for a few excruciating minutes while he tried to find a place to turn around. When he'd gotten back in sight of the place, Cortland's men were already setting the explosives. Which meant they still believed she was inside as well.

So if she'd gotten out of the place, how had she done it?

He pulled his burner phone out of his pocket and turned it on. The display stared back at him, daring him to make a call that could cost him his freedom, maybe for good.

But it was a chance he had to take.

He dialed the number of the Bitterwood Police Department and started to ask for Ivy Hawkins when movement to the left of the truck caught his eye. Someone was walking through the grove of young trees about fifty yards away, moving with stealth. He caught a glimpse of a black jacket between the long limbs of pine saplings that grew on the hillside, then a flash of long dark hair twisted up in a messy ponytail.

His heart skipped a beat.

DELILAH FALTERED TO a halt in the middle of the pine grove, wiping her eyes. The cold, combined with the lingering effects of the tear gas, conspired to blind her as she tried to make her way silently to the edge of the lumberyard property. She'd spent the time it took to unscrew the metal grille from the tunnel entrance trying to figure out the best way to confront Cortland, settling on the simplest answer possible.

Nobody expected a visit from a dead woman. And if she could make her stand against Cortland in public, surrounded by ordinary people going about their workday, buying lumber and supplies, she just might be able to walk out of there alive. Someone would call the police, of course. But that was good. She wanted the police to come. If she had a phone on her, she'd call the police herself.

If the spy watch had worked as it was supposed to, she had Nolan Cavanaugh's testimony on video. And even if she didn't, Cavanaugh had given her names and locations that good investigators might be able to mine to find the truth.

She also had her own testimony about what had happened to her when she tried to talk to Cortland. She'd been locked up, gassed, kidnapped and damn near killed. She could testify to all of those acts. There was a pile of rubble a mile up the road to back her up.

She took a few steadying breaths and pushed away from the pine tree trunk she'd been leaning against, ready to face the dragon in his lair.

But a snap of a twig behind her froze her in place.

The hair on the back of her neck bristled. Her muscles bunched, ready for fight or flight, whichever might be required.

"You look damn good for someone who just blew up in a warehouse."

Brand's voice, low and warm just a few inches behind her, made her knees buckle. She grabbed the tree trunk to keep from falling and turned around, half-afraid she'd imagined his voice.

But he was there, dust-covered and bleeding from one shoulder. His dark hair looked gray, and his face was grimy. But his blue eyes were clear and blazing as he stared across the narrow gap between them.

"I told you to stay at the cabin," she said, her voice raspy.

"I'm afraid I'm about as good at following orders as you are." He took a step toward her, his face crinkling as if he was on the brink of breaking down. She'd never seen him look so fragile, not even when they'd lost Jim Fielding. His lips pressed into a thin line, as if he was struggling to keep his emotions in check.

"Brand?"

"I saw the place explode."

"How did you—?"

"I saw them throw you in the shed, then come out with the box. The tracker showed you must be in the box, so I followed the truck they put you in." He reached out slowly, as if he needed to touch her, to reassure himself she was real and not just a mirage.

She caught his hand, twining her fingers through his. He stared at her, lips trembling. Then, so quickly it made her breath catch, he pulled her to him, his grip as strong as steel.

Chapter Eighteen

"You can't just walk in there and confront him," Brand said, panic twisting in his gut at the thought of her putting herself back in danger after he'd come so close to losing her.

But Delilah's squared jaw told him he was fighting a losing battle. "Hand me the computer."

They were in Liz's truck—Delilah had wanted to download the video she'd recorded in the tunnel.

He handed her the backpack where he'd put the tablet. "I'm not even sure why I brought it—I guess I didn't want to leave it back at the cabin, in case we had to make a run for it."

"Good thing you did."

"Will this give us the evidence we need?"

"It's better than nothing," she said. "I hope we can find Cavanaugh so he can provide testimony himself."

"Is it enough?" he asked as she started the download.

"It's a lot," she said.

As he watched, she held her breath and hit the play button on the video player. A grainy, dark image flickered to life. A sandy-haired man, grimy and scared-looking, spoke to the camera.

"My name is Nolan Cavanaugh. I was a witness last year in federal court against former White House chief of staff Katrina Hilliard, former Energy Secretary Morris Gamble and several of their coconspirators in an attempt to use extortion, duress and murder to influence Congress in a vote on a global energy treaty. I was sent into a federal witness protection program, where I stumbled on an anarchist group called Black Banner that was working to undermine an energy-research project called the Devonian Project."

Brand listened as Cavanaugh explained how he recognized remnants of the hacker group that had aided the now defunct Espera Group in their attempt to seize control of global energy production. "Black Banner's aim is global anarchy, the complete destruction of civil society and any rules that govern it. It was their reason for helping Espera Group, convinced that global control of energy would be the beginning of the end of the United States and their global hegemony."

Brand glanced at Delilah. She rolled her eyes, making him smile. Of course, right about now, just the sight of her grimy face, so alive and alert, was enough to make him want to laugh aloud.

"They found unexpected allies in a Virginia militia group called the Blue Ridge Infantry, a ragtag band of white-power and antigovernment radicals who discovered their aims and those of Black Banner were more aligned than either group expected. But neither group would have been able to do much more than make some noise and print a few pamphlets if they hadn't met a man named Wayne Cortland."

Cavanaugh outlined everything he knew, naming names, rattling off a series of connections that made Brand's mind reel. "I've been trying to figure out where Cortland keeps his books. He's far too organized to be able to keep all the balls in the air without some means of record keeping. But I haven't been able to get far enough into the organization to find where he'd store those records." A moment later, the video ended.

Delilah looked at Brand. "Does it help?"

"Not as much as the actual records would. But Cavanaugh gives us a lot of names to work with that we didn't have before."

"It doesn't prove your innocence."

"It may help. One of the names Cavanaugh mentions is Hogan Lombard."

Delilah nodded. "One of the Blue Ridge Infantry members."

"Hogan Lombard's name came up in Liz's address book when the police were investigating. He'd been one of her informants, according to her notes."

"Or maybe he was just pretending to be."

"If we can place Lombard anywhere near her place the night she died, it would be a damned good start."

"What if it's not enough?"

He reached out and slid a loose lock of hair behind her ear, wishing he could promise her that everything was going to be okay. But she was right. Though it was a start, there was no guarantee the authorities would see things the way he and Delilah did.

"That's a chance we have to take," he said firmly, dropping his hand back to his side. "It's time to come in from the cold."

She looked at him, her dark eyes fathomless. "And then what?"

He realized what she was asking. And there were a dozen damned good reasons why he could distance himself from her, put up walls to keep her out of his mess. But he couldn't bring himself to do it. Not this time.

Never again.

He reached across the truck cab and cradled her face between his hands. "Whatever happens, I'm going to find a way to be with you. If that's what you want."

She closed her fingers over his, squeezing them. "Even if it means never going back to the FBI?"

He laughed softly. "I don't think there's much point in

doing that, do you? You know how things are at the bureau. Even if I'm fully exonerated, this is a black mark that won't go away."

"But if you could, would you?"

It was a fair question. One that deserved an honest answer.

So what *was* the honest answer? If he could erase all the strikes against him and go back to the FBI with a clean slate, would he?

It wasn't even a hard choice, he realized with surprise. "No," he said. "I wouldn't go back."

"Even if I went with you?"

"Would you?"

"If that's what it took," she admitted, her gaze helpless.

He kissed her. "Only if it was what we both wanted. And I don't think that's what either of us wants anymore, is it?"

She shook her head. "But we're going to get you out of this mess."

"I know."

She threaded her fingers through his and leaned up to kiss him, a sweet, hot kiss that made his head spin a little. "I love you, Adam Brand. I think I probably always have."

He laughed softly. "Never thought I'd hear you admit that, Hammond."

Her brow creased. "You're making me regret it already."

Pressing his lips against her furrowed brow, he pulled her into his arms across the truck's bench seat until he felt her heart pounding against his chest. "I love you, too. From the moment you stepped foot in my office, I was utterly lost. I'm just sorry it took this long to admit to myself that I don't want to live a life without you in it."

"So whatever happens, we're in this together?" She pulled back and looked at him, equal parts fear and joy in her eyes.

"We're going to have ourselves one of those happily ever afters," he promised. "You believe that, don't you?"

Her lips curved in a smile. "You know, I believe I do."

THEY LEFT THE Camaro at Liz Vaughn's cabin and took the truck, since nobody would be looking for it. The drive from Travisville to Bitterwood took a little over three hours, with a stop for food on the way. The two of them made a bedraggled sight when they walked through the front doors of the Bitterwood Police Department and asked to see Detective Ivy Hawkins.

"Son of a bitch" was Ivy's terse response when she recognized Brand's face from the wanted poster hanging on the bulletin board behind the front desk. She took Brand into custody without incident, told Delilah to stay put and hauled her new prisoner back to holding.

Twenty minutes later, Sutton Calhoun came through the front door of the station and sat in the empty chair next to Delilah in the waiting area. "Ivy called."

"Where's my mother?"

"Travis Cooper is with her. Jesse sent him up here to give us extra backup."

Good old Jesse, Delilah thought, wondering if she'd been a fool to quit Cooper Security for a job in Bitterwood. The Coopers were the best kind of people, men and women who'd do the right thing without counting the costs.

"How's she doing?"

"Day eight without a drink. I've never seen her look better."

"Good." Delilah felt tears burning the backs of her eyes. She told herself it was the aftereffects of the tear gas.

"You look like hell."

"Well, I've been tear-gassed and nearly blown up."

"You've been with Brand the whole time?"

She nodded. "Is that common knowledge?"

"Not really. I just know you."

She looked at him. Even through the obvious concern for her evident in his expression, he looked happy. She'd known him most of her life, and never before could she remember seeing him look so happy. "When are you and Ivy going to make it legal?"

"As soon as we can get Seth and Rachel back in town safely. We wanted the two of them and you to be there. And Ivy's mom, of course."

"Wouldn't miss it," she said with a forced smile. Her cheeks hurt from the effort.

Sutton put his arm around her, something else he didn't normally do. "It's going to be okay, Dee. We'll figure this out."

"I need to talk to Ivy, but I don't want to draw too much attention to myself yet. Brand's got a video on the computer in his backpack. I have to make sure someone sees it. Can you get word to Ivy?"

"I'm sure they took his backpack when he was booked. They'll search it and find the computer."

Her eyes narrowed. "Who would have it?"

Sutton gave her an odd look. "Probably the properties officer."

"Where do I find him?"

Sutton picked up on her alarm, but he didn't ask questions. He just directed her down the hall. "Third door on the right."

She walked down the hall, ignoring the desk sergeant when he asked where she was going. Pushing through the door Sutton had indicated, she strode down the corridor to the room at the far end, where a clerk at the window was talking to a burly, dark-haired man holding Brand's backpack. Both men looked up at the sound of her footsteps approaching.

She looked at the dark-haired man, unsurprised to recognize the captain of detectives, Glen Rayburn. "Captain." She folded her arms in front of her, letting her thumb brush across the record button on her watch.

Rayburn's smile was downright vicious. "I tried to tell the chief you'd be trouble. And look here. Aiding and abetting a fugitive."

"I brought the fugitive in," she said flatly.

"You think I don't know you've been helping him?"

"Really. You know?" She cocked her head. "How would you know that?"

Rayburn's eyes flickered a moment. "I'm not stupid."

"Or maybe you have a buddy in Travisville, Virginia, who keeps you informed of things he's doing so you can be sure to look the other way?" Delilah cocked her head. "I kept wondering why a police captain couldn't look at four clearly connected murders and see that they were the work of the same perpetrator. Unless you didn't want to see it."

"You're treading on dangerous ground, Ms. Hammond."

"Why? Because I'm too close to the truth?"

"Because people who cross me don't make it very far on this force."

She shrugged. "And then I couldn't figure out why Cortland's men would target my brother."

"Maybe he was targeting the Davenport girl," Rayburn said.

"But he went after my brother's car, not Rachel's."

"He could know they're involved."

Delilah narrowed her eyes. "You know what I find curious?"

The captain's eyes darkened with contempt. "I'm dying to know what you find curious."

"I find it curious you haven't asked me who Cortland is."

Rayburn's expression faltered. He shot a glance at the

property-room clerk, who stared back at him with a furrowed brow. "Who's Cortland?" Rayburn asked belatedly.

Delilah shook her head. "I've suspected for a while that whoever was behind the Bitterwood murders had help from someone in the police department. But you know when I figured it out for sure?"

Rayburn's eyes narrowed further, but he didn't speak.

"Where were you yesterday around twelve-thirty?"

"In my office."

"If I ask around, is that the answer I'll get?"

"Absolutely."

"And if I were to get a subpoena for your cell-phone records, would I find a call from Wayne Cortland?"

Rayburn looked scared. "What are you implying?"

"I've spoken to maybe seven people since I returned to Bitterwood. My family, Rachel Davenport, Ivy Hawkins, Sutton Calhoun, Chief Albertson—and you. You're the only people who would be able to recognize my voice on hearing it."

"So?" Rayburn was sweating now, reassuring Delilah that she was on the right track.

"So, someone told Wayne Cortland that the woman who called his lumberyard yesterday shortly after noon was me."

"What makes you think that?"

"Because he was ready for me. He had me abducted and gassed and tried to blow me up in one of his warehouses."

"Yet here you are." Rayburn tried to sound tough, but he'd turned a pasty color and looked as if he wanted to run away as fast and as far as he could.

"Yes. Here I am." She looked at the backpack, wondering if telling him about Cavanaugh's recorded statement would prod him into doing something foolish.

No matter. She still had the confession on her watch. As long as she had the watch, he could destroy anything in the backpack he wanted.

Maybe they could even use that to set Rayburn up.

Before she could wrap up their discussion, however, Sutton Calhoun came walking down the hall, his expression grim. Delilah watched his approach, her heart in her throat.

Had something happened to Brand? Was she wrong about Rayburn? Was there someone else in the Bitterwood Police Department on Wayne Cortland's payroll?

"There's a news report you need to see," Sutton told her, sliding a look of dislike toward Rayburn.

"What is it?"

Sutton nodded for her to come with him.

She spared one last look at Rayburn and followed Sutton out to the front, where a handful of police and support personnel stood in a ring around the television in the waiting area.

A Knoxville news station was showing a live feed from a station out of the TriCities area, where a news helicopter was hovering over a massive fire. "Witnesses report there was a massive explosion in the lumberyard office, spreading debris and fire into the lumberyard itself. So far, there has been no estimate of casualties, although emergency crews from as far away as Abingdon have begun to arrive in Travisville to back up the local crews, suggesting casualties may be significant."

Delilah dropped into the nearest chair, staring at the raging fire on the television screen. What had once been the Cortland Lumber showroom was a roaring inferno. Lumber, once stacked in neat rows in front of the office, lay shattered and strewn across the yard, dotting the ground with dozens of small, outlying fires.

"When did it happen?" she asked Sutton, who stood beside her, his hand on her shoulder.

"About an hour ago."

Not long after she and Brand had gotten away.

If she'd gone to face down Cortland as she'd originally planned, she might very well be dead.

THE HOLDING CELL was small but mostly clean, a sign that the Bitterwood jail saw only light and sporadic use. Brand had the whole cell block to himself and was amused that the sound of footsteps ringing through the cell block came as a relief.

The uniformed guard walking down the cell-block corridor was of average height and build, with a sandy beard, sharp hazel eyes and a look of single-minded determination. If Brand hadn't recognized the newcomer, he'd have been certain he was about to be assassinated, for the bearded man had a distinctly dangerous air. Even upon recognizing his visitor, he wasn't sure he was going to make it out of the Bitterwood jail alive.

CIA operatives like Alexander Quinn had a way of leaving a trail of bodies in their wake.

"Most days, I try to be strictly professional," Quinn murmured, stopping outside Brand's cell. "But I must admit, I do enjoy seeing an FBI agent behind bars."

Brand didn't rise to the spy's bait. "Did you arrange all this? Have you been using Cortland and his operation for some twisted plot of yours?"

Quinn's lip curled. "I realize you don't have a very good opinion of me, or people in the agency in general, but I'm on your side in this one. Cortland was a very bad man."

Brand narrowed his eyes. "Was?"

"An hour ago, someone detonated a series of incendiary bombs in the offices of Cortland Lumber. The place is currently going up in flames."

"Someone?"

Quinn's lips flattened with annoyance. "No one with

whom I'm affiliated, I assure you. Innocent people died in that attack."

"Wouldn't be the first time."

"One of my operatives was almost certainly killed as well."

The pain in Quinn's eyes looked genuine. Brand almost felt sorry for the manipulative bastard. "Would this operative happen to be the American radical formerly known as Sinclair Solano?"

Quinn didn't seem surprised by Brand's question. "Yes."

"You think he was killed in the blast?"

"I haven't heard from him since he contacted me to tell me about your meeting with him at the lumberyard. But in case he made it, it's vital that you don't tell anyone you saw him today."

"What are the two of you up to?"

"I can't tell you. But I will tell you this. Sinclair Solano isn't one of the bad guys. Not anymore, and not for a long time."

Brand didn't try to argue with Quinn, though he suspected the CIA agent's concept of good and bad might not coincide precisely with his own. Instead, he asked, "Are you sure Cortland was in his office when it blew up?"

"Every indication is that he was killed in the explosion," Quinn answered with a hint of feral satisfaction. "There'll be an investigation. DNA comparisons. We'll know, sooner or later."

"Why are you telling me this?"

"Because I'm going to do whatever I can to make sure you're cleared of the charges against you."

Brand shot him a look. "If you were capable of that, why haven't you done it before now?"

"The CIA is choosy about what operations they run on American soil."

Brand swallowed a snort. "You wanted Cortland out of business."

"I wanted Cortland to stop running guns, drugs and terrorists out of South America into this country."

"So we were right about the kinds of things he was up to."

"You knew he was planning a cyberattack on the Oak Ridge National Laboratory, I presume."

"We suspected as much."

"You know they were trying to neutralize the research of the Devonian Project, then."

"You know, Quinn, if you ever shared what you know with the rest of the country, we might be better off."

"I told you, the CIA—"

"Why don't you just quit the CIA and start your own detective agency? Then you could investigate whatever you wanted without having to twist yourself into knots."

Quinn looked thoughtful for a second, then he started to walk away.

"That's it?" Brand called. "That's all you have to say?"

Quinn didn't answer. But he jerked to a halt when a loud sound filtered in from somewhere not far from the cell block. His hand automatically closed over the service revolver holstered at his side.

"That was a gunshot," Brand said.

Quinn looked over his shoulder. "Yes, it was."

A SHARP CRACKING sound came from somewhere nearby. For a moment, Delilah thought the sound had come from the television, until several of the police officers standing around started running.

She followed, even though she wasn't armed, her heart pounding with terror that, somehow, someone had gotten to Brand right here in the police station.

But the police bypassed the door to the holding cells and

ran down the hall to the detectives' communal office instead. Delilah spotted Antoine Parsons standing in front of the open door of the captain's office, his expression shell-shocked and bleak.

Delilah didn't have to take another step into the room to know what had happened. The faces of the police officers who looked into Captain Rayburn's office made clear what had happened.

Rayburn had found a way out of the mess after all.

Epilogue

"So, what now?"

Rain drummed the roof of Delilah's house, lulling her into a light doze. Brand's soft question roused her back to full consciousness. She turned onto her side and looked at him, smiling at the sight of him finally back in her bed where he belonged. "I need to give Bitterwood P.D. a final answer. They've held the detective position open for a month to give us time to deal with the fallout, but now that you've been cleared, they need my answer."

"It's a police force in upheaval," Brand warned, rolling over to look at her. "That could be a plus or a minus."

"It's definitely more of a challenge now. Chief Albertson turned in his resignation this morning, so there'll be a big hiring push to get a new chief. I'm sure they're going to look for someone from outside the county, someone with a good reputation. Plus, today I heard the D.A.'s office is going to assign a public integrity officer to the department for the foreseeable future."

Brand grimaced. "That's even worse than having Internal Affairs nosing around."

"I know. It's necessary, though."

"True." He gave her a thoughtful look. "And you still want to take the job, knowing all that?"

"Yeah. I do. Are you good with that?"

He touched her face. "I'm good with anything you want. As long as you want me."

She kissed him. "Always."

They shifted positions, spooning under the warm covers. Brand had shaved his beard; she almost missed the rasp of his stubble against her skin. "I've had an interesting job offer," he murmured against her shoulder.

"And you're just now telling me?"

"I wasn't sure we'd be staying in Bitterwood."

"So it's something local?"

"Yeah. Alexander Quinn has retired from the CIA."

"You're kidding me." Delilah had crossed paths with the CIA agent more than once during her work with Cooper Security. She'd always figured Alexander Quinn would go out in a blaze of gunfire in some war-torn country. Retirement had never figured into her imaginings. "And this has something to do with your job offer? You're going to become a spy?"

"No. Quinn's just bought a big building in Purgatory, Tennessee. Turns out that's where the old bastard grew up."

"He wasn't spawned, fully grown, from some alien space pod?"

Brand gave her hip a little slap. "Well, he says that's why he's opening his detective agency in Purgatory. Could be a lie, I suppose."

"He's going to be a small-town P.I.?"

"Appears so. He wants me to join him as his agent-training coordinator. Apparently he plans to build the agency from the ground up. Pick his own candidates for investigators and security guards. But the CIA's training methods don't translate well for civilian investigations."

"And that's where you come in?"

"What do you think? He's offering me a pretty significant percentage of the profits if I come in from the beginning.

Purgatory is a ten-minute drive from here—I could hardly ask for a better commute."

"What do you want to do?" she asked, turning to face him.

"I want to do it," he admitted. "Because I could certainly use some extra money about now."

"Yeah?" She arched her eyebrow at him. "Why's that?"

He rolled over and opened the bedside-table drawer. She half expected him to pull out another condom, but instead, he came away with a small velvet ring box.

Her heart skipped a beat.

He opened it to reveal a diamond solitaire flanked by a pair of small emeralds. "Make an honest man of me, Delilah Hammond?"

She stared at the ring, then back at his face, surprised by the anxiety she saw blazing in his blue eyes. "Did you think I'd say no?"

His lips curved slightly. "I've learned not to assume I'm ever going to know what you'll say or do."

She laughed. "I guess I can't argue with that."

"So?" he prodded, pulling the ring from its velvet bed.

She held out her left hand. "Just as long as we're clear on one thing."

He slipped the ring on her finger, lifting her hand to his lips to kiss her knuckles. "What's that?"

"No fancy wedding, no 'obey' in the vows and we shoot anyone who tries to tie tin cans to my Camaro."

Brand pulled her flush to his body, revealing just how happy he was that she'd said yes to his proposal. "Deal."

* * * * *

*Look for more books in award-winning author
Paula Graves's miniseries* BITTERWOOD, P.D. *in 2014,
wherever Harlequin Intrigue books are sold!*

REQUEST YOUR FREE BOOKS!
2 FREE NOVELS PLUS 2 FREE GIFTS!

HARLEQUIN

INTRIGUE

BREATHTAKING ROMANTIC SUSPENSE

YES! Please send me 2 FREE Harlequin Intrigue® novels and my 2 FREE gifts (gifts are worth about $10). After receiving them, if I don't wish to receive any more books, I can return the shipping statement marked "cancel." If I don't cancel, I will receive 6 brand-new novels every month and be billed just $4.74 per book in the U.S. or $5.24 per book in Canada. That's a savings of at least 14% off the cover price! It's quite a bargain! Shipping and handling is just 50¢ per book in the U.S. and 75¢ per book in Canada.* I understand that accepting the 2 free books and gifts places me under no obligation to buy anything. I can always return a shipment and cancel at any time. Even if I never buy another book, the two free books and gifts are mine to keep forever.

182/382 HDN F42N

Name	(PLEASE PRINT)	
Address		Apt. #
City	State/Prov.	Zip/Postal Code

Signature (if under 18, a parent or guardian must sign)

Mail to the **Harlequin® Reader Service:**
IN U.S.A.: P.O. Box 1867, Buffalo, NY 14240-1867
IN CANADA: P.O. Box 609, Fort Erie, Ontario L2A 5X3
**Are you a subscriber to Harlequin Intrigue books
and want to receive the larger-print edition?
Call 1-800-873-8635 or visit www.ReaderService.com.**

* Terms and prices subject to change without notice. Prices do not include applicable taxes. Sales tax applicable in N.Y. Canadian residents will be charged applicable taxes. Offer not valid in Quebec. This offer is limited to one order per household. Not valid for current subscribers to Harlequin Intrigue books. All orders subject to credit approval. Credit or debit balances in a customer's account(s) may be offset by any other outstanding balance owed by or to the customer. Please allow 4 to 6 weeks for delivery. Offer available while quantities last.

Your Privacy—The Harlequin® Reader Service is committed to protecting your privacy. Our Privacy Policy is available online at www.ReaderService.com or upon request from the Harlequin Reader Service.

We make a portion of our mailing list available to reputable third parties that offer products we believe may interest you. If you prefer that we not exchange your name with third parties, or if you wish to clarify or modify your communication preferences, please visit us at www.ReaderService.com/consumerchoice or write to us at Harlequin Reader Service Preference Service, P.O. Box 9062, Buffalo, NY 14269. Include your complete name and address.

HI13R

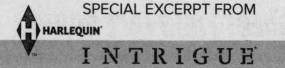
She flashed an overly bright smile and handed him a
passport. "That's you, right?"

He opened it and, startled, gazed up at her. "Who are you?"

"You know me," she murmured, leaning closer. "Thomas."

His eyes went wide as he recognized her voice under
the disguise.

"I need you." The words were out, full of more truth than
she cared to admit regarding their past, present and, quite
possibly, their immediate future.

He nodded once, all business, and fell in beside her as she
headed toward an employee access. She refused to look back,
though she could feel Grant closing in as the door locked
behind them.

"This way."

"Tell me what's going on, Jo."

She ignored the ripple of awareness that followed his using
her given name. It wasn't the reaction she'd expected. Thomas

always treated everyone with efficient professionalism. Except for that one notable, extremely personal, incident years ago.

"I'll tell you everything just as soon as we're out of here." She checked her watch. They had less than five minutes before the cabbie she'd paid to wait left in search of another fare. "Keep up. We have to get out of the area before the roads are closed." She'd taken precautions, given herself options, but no one could prepare for a freak blizzard.

"Are you in trouble?"

"Yes." On one too many levels, she realized. But it was too late to back out now. If she didn't follow through, someone more objective would take over the investigation. Based on what she'd seen, she didn't think that was a good idea.

Moving forward, she hoped some deep-seated instinct would kick in, making him curious enough to cooperate with her.

"Jo, wait."

Would the day ever come when his voice didn't create that shiver of anticipation? "No time."

"I need an explanation."

"And I'll give you one when we're away from the airport."

Can Jo be trusted or is it a trap?
Then again, nothing is too dangerous for these agents…
except falling in love.

Don't miss
Bridal Armor
by Debra Webb
Book one in the
COLBY AGENCY: THE SPECIALISTS SERIES

Available August 20, edge-of-your-seat romance,
only from Harlequin® Intrigue®!

SADDLE UP AND READ 'EM!

Looking for another great Western read? Check out these September reads from the SUSPENSE category!

COWBOY REDEMPTION by Elle James
Covert Cowboys
Harlequin Intrigue

MOST ELIGIBLE SPY by Dana Marton
HQ: Texas
Harlequin Intrigue

Look for these great Western reads and more available wherever books are sold or visit
www.Harlequin.com/Westerns